Some Like It Haute

SOME LIKE IT HAUTE

Book 4 in the Killer Fashion Mystery Series

A Polyester Press Mystery

First published 2015

Copyright © 2021, 2019, 2015, Diane Vallere

e-ISBN: 9781939197979

print ISBN: 9781939197986

PRAISE FOR THE SAMANTHA KIDD MYSTERIES:

"...the book is enriched by the author's cleverly phrased prose and convincing characterization. The surprise ending will satisfy and delight many mystery fans. A diverting mystery that offers laughs and chills." -*Kirkus Reviews*

"an impressive cozy mystery from a promising author." -*Mystery Tribune*

"Designer Dirty Laundry shows that even the toughest crime is no match for a sleuth in fishnet stockings who knows her way around the designer department. A delightful debut." -Kris Neri, Lefty Award-Nominated author of *Revenge For Old Times' Sake*

"Combining fashion and fatalities, Diane Vallere pens a winning debut mystery...a sleek and stylish read." -Ellen Byerrum, National Bestselling author of the Crime of Fashion mysteries

"Vallere once again brings her knowledgeable fashion skills to the forefront, along with comedy, mystery, and a saucy romance. *Buyer, Beware* did not disappoint!" -*Chick Lit Plus*

"Fashion is always at the forefront, but never at the cost of excellent writing, humorous dialogue, or a compelling story." -*Kings River Life*

"A captivating new mystery voice, Vallere has stitched together haute couture and murder in a stylish mystery. Dirty Laundry has never been so engrossing!" -Krista Davis, *New York Times* Bestselling Author of The Domestic Diva Mysteries

"Samantha Kidd is an engaging amateur sleuth." -*Mysterious Reviews*

"It keeps you at the edge of your seat. I love the description of clothes in this book...if you love fashion, pick this up!" -*Los Angeles Mamma Blog*

"Diane Vallere takes the reader through this cozy mystery with her signature wit and humor." -Mary Marks, *NY Journal of Books*

"The Samantha Kidd Mysteries continue to be completely fun and entertaining." -*Carstairs Considers*

a killer fashion mystery

Some Like It Haute

DIANE VALLERE

Polyester Press

READING, PA

To Cynthia, who taught me far more than what I needed to know to be a buyer.

INTRODUCTION

There are three things you need to know about me:

1. I have questionable judgment

2. I can't walk away from a challenge

3. I'm not as tough as I pretend to be

If you consider these three things you'll start to understand why I agreed to help Amanda Ries, my ex-boyfriend's maybe-former-girlfriend, with her runway show (*questionable judgment*). You'll understand why, after I was assaulted in the parking lot outside of said runway show and warned to mind my own business, I was more determined than ever to figure out what was going on (*that walking-away-from-a-challenge thing*). And you might even see how hard it is for me to put on a brave face while inside, I'm still torn up over my recent breakup with Nick Taylor. (*Six weeks, four days, and a handful of hours, not that I'm counting.*)

Nick was the one who suggested that Amanda hire me. I have over a decade of experience in the fashion industry, and Amanda was lucky to get me, breakup baggage notwithstanding. While working for her, I spent my days at Warehouse Five acting as liaison between the powers that be while juggling mundane tasks of the "we're out of Coke Zero" variety.

And then Amanda fired me. Fired by the maybe-former girlfriend? Not. Acceptable. I should have let it go and walked away, but I didn't. (see point #2). Instead, I finagled a date with a suitably hot photographer and attended her runway show as a patron, watching from the sidelines while one of the outfits burst into flames on the runway.

Fast forward to today. I'd like to say I spent my morning enjoying a cup of coffee before heading out to do some personal shopping for a client. But I'd be lying. In the past twenty-four hours I've chopped off my hair, revisited a crime scene, made out with the hot photographer, and witnessed another fire. I've found an unlikely ally in the local police detective, whose hands are tied in the investigation because a local arson investigator is calling the shots. And even though nobody else is asking the question, I'd like to know who attacked me, so I'm conducting my own investigation of all parties involved. Which, among others, includes Amanda, the maybe-former girlfriend.

This is that story.

1

PAPER PAJAMAS

The smell told me I wasn't at home. Before I opened my eyes and saw the two concerned faces staring at me, before I heard the sounds of the monitors and medical equipment that sat close by, before I felt the scratchy sheets on the bed, I was assaulted by the scent of antiseptic cherry cleanser.

The faces were familiar. There was Eddie Adams, my close friend and confidant. And behind him, diverting her eyes, was Amanda Ries.

Not a confidant. Not even a sometimes friend.

She was my ex-boyfriend's maybe-former girlfriend.

Eddie and Amanda looked at me with a mixture of concern, fear, and embarrassment.

"She's awake," Eddie said when my eyes focused on him. "Dude, are you okay?"

I scanned the room, taking in the medical equipment, heart-rate monitor machines, and curtain that had been pulled back so I could see my visitors. I glanced down at my outfit.

Paper pajamas.

"Is this a hospital room?" I asked.

"Yes," Eddie said.

"Am I the patient?"

"Yes."

"Did I come here in an ambulance?"

"Yes."

"Then I don't think I'm okay."

Amanda burst into tears.

———

TWENTY-FOUR HOURS EARLIER...

Ridiculously tall and thin girls surrounded me. Ridiculously tall and thin women. Ridiculously tall and thin *something*. They were so unlike the people I usually spent time with that I didn't know what to call them.

They were models.

They pranced around in stick-on bras and barely-there panties, waiting to be pinned and taped and glued and tied into the fashions that they would wear at the upcoming Amanda Ries runway show. Tonight was the dress rehearsal to check fittings, practice walking the runway, and generally make sure nothing had been left to chance. It was Fashion Week—or the closest thing that existed outside of New York City. Thanks to its proximity to the Big Apple, our little town of Ribbon, Pennsylvania, hosted its own version of Fashion Week, often convincing buyers to make the two-hour trek and check out the talent. It didn't matter that we weren't in the fashion capital of the country but rather about 150 miles west. Fashion Week adjacent, if you will.

"Miss Kidd, where do we go after we're done with our fittings?" one of the waifish models asked. A flashbulb popped in my face. I blinked several times, trying to restore my eyesight. "Miss Kidd?" she asked again.

"It's Samantha, not Miss Kidd," I lectured. I wasn't that much older than they were. Well, maybe I was, but admitting your age at a fashion show wasn't unlike telling your herd of cattle that you were the weak one. I pointed down a narrow hallway with walls covered in bulletin boards. "Last room on the right."

I felt a tug on my sleeve. "Excuse me, ma'am?" said a little-girl voice. "I think there's been a mistake with my second look."

Ma'am? She couldn't be talking to me. I looked at the model. Wide blue eyes, long blond hair, and a body of angles and bones. Sixteen years old was my best guess, only because anything younger would have been illegal.

I climbed up on a small step stool. "Can I have everyone's attention?" I hollered. Someone shushed, and the crowd quieted down. "I am Samantha. Not Miss Kidd, not ma'am. If you have a question for me, and you expect me to answer, you need to call me Samantha."

I hopped down from the step stool and pushed it under the nearest table.

"She's turning this place into a circus," said a voice next to me. An attractive man in an unstructured black-and-white tweed jacket and a porkpie hat stood next to me. His thick gray hair seemed out of place against his youthful olive skin. "Warehouse Five used to be an artists' studio. Now it's a joke."

"You don't think fashion design is a form of art?" I asked.

He watched the models. "It's a money-making machine. Look at these people. Acting like any of this is important. They're clothes. They'll be in style for a couple of months, and then everybody will forget about them. That's not art." He turned to me. "Are you part of the problem?"

"I'm here to help out, if that's what you mean. Samantha Kidd," I said, holding out my hand.

"Santangelo Toma."

"You're an artist?"

He nodded. "I do portraits and nudes. My studio is down the hall. Ever since these clowns showed up, I can barely hear myself think. It's an insult to the rest of us that they've been allowed to take over."

"The show's tomorrow night, and then it'll all be done."

"For good, hopefully. I started a petition to make sure something like this doesn't happen again." He glared at the models and then turned around and left.

One more stressor for Amanda. The last thing a designer would want in the panicked days before her first major fashion show was to learn the tenants of the building wanted her out.

The shy stick figure who'd called me ma'am was still next to me. She tugged on my sleeve again. "I'm sorry to bother you, but I think there's been a mistake."

The outfit in question was a silver lamé kimono. It hung open, exposing her skinny torso and flesh-colored panties. There wasn't a high price placed on modesty backstage at a runway show, with models often parading around half clothed, but this girl didn't have any goods to show off even if someone was interested. She held her arms out to the side, palms up, and raised her shoulders. Her hands were completely hidden by sleeves that were too long for her limbs, sleeves that hung down to the floor.

I sighed. "Let's go ask someone." I looked around, over, and under bust forms, mannequins, and rolling rods, until I found an imposing black man who stood head and shoulders above the (ridiculously tall) models. He had a tailor's tape draped over his shoulders and was dressed in a vest and trousers over a pressed dress shirt and navy blue plaid tie. We headed his way.

"Can you help her? This kimono doesn't seem to fit right," I said.

A few of the girls laughed amongst themselves. The man asked, "Are you Harper?"

The model nodded. The man turned to me. "All of the samples have been fitted and approved. That is how it's going down the runway. Harper was specifically requested to wear it."

The other models snickered again. Harper's eyes filled with tears, and she turned away from them.

I didn't have the energy for this. If Amanda wanted Harper to wear the oversized and poorly fitting kimono, then who was I to override that decision? Just the unassuming ex-girlfriend of the designer's maybe-former boyfriend. But I didn't have time to think about that. I had a model in the throes of an emotional breakdown and no Twizzlers in sight.

"If you have a problem, then you have to ask Amanda," the man said. "It's her show."

Again, I scanned the warehouse for the designer. The man pointed toward the back of the stage. Amanda was partially visible. She was talking to a person I couldn't see. Amanda's straight black hair hung in a thick, glossy sheath between her shoulder blades. She ran her hand over the top, smoothing strands that had probably never been out of place in their life.

I bet nobody called her ma'am.

I headed toward Amanda with Harper close to my heels. When we reached the designer, I saw who was on the other side of the conversation. Amanda's financial partner, a six-foot-tall Amazonian named Tiny Anderson. Tiny, as I'd come to learn, wore some version of the same outfit everyday: white oxford shirt, gray sweater, dark-wash men's jeans, and brogues. Both unisex and unflattering, her uniform served the dual purpose of letting her blend into the crowd while being sure that nobody mistook her for anybody else.

I waited for an appropriate pause in their conversation so I could interrupt.

"When is Nick getting here with the shoes?" Tiny asked.

"Nick isn't bringing the shoes tonight," Amanda said.

"We still have to do a hem check." Tiny gestured toward the models with a hand holding several spools of metallic thread. A row of silver straight pins lined the hem of her sweater. "I thought he knew how important it was that we had everything here for the run-through." Tiny glared down at Amanda.

"Nick didn't want to show up today because of—" She stopped mid-sentence. The two of them turned and looked directly at me.

This had been one of the worst months of my life. And that's counting the times when I'd happened upon dead bodies, stood face-to-face with murderers, and almost gotten killed. This was worse than all of that.

Somehow, after breaking up with my shoe-designer boyfriend Nick Taylor, I'd gotten myself in the position of helping his ex-girlfriend Amanda Ries coordinate her runway show.

2

SHOW NO SIGNS OF WEAKNESS

BREAKUP RULE #1: SHOW NO SIGNS OF WEAKNESS TO YOUR ex's friends. That's why I arrived, on time, on that first day of scheduling. Amanda had hired me for my fashion experience and professionalism, and I was prepared to bring it. I wasn't going to give her fuel for any fodder about me.

But it was painfully obvious that Amanda wouldn't be singing my praises to anybody. Her show was being railroaded because Nick wanted to avoid me.

"I'm sorry to interrupt," I said. I thought it best to pretend I hadn't overheard them. "Harper has a problem with the sleeves on her kimono. They're too long. There must have been a mistake."

Tiny was the one to talk. "We picked every model's looks based on their measurements and coloring. There is no room for error, and considering these decisions were made by us"—she used her hand to make a sweeping gesture that included herself and Amanda—"I highly doubt there's been any mistake. Remind the girl she's supposed to be a professional, and that she has about five seconds to decide if she can do that before we replace her."

"But look at this," I said. I grabbed one of Harper's wrists and held her arm out. The fabric at the bottom of the sleeve pooled onto the ground. I turned toward Amanda. "Is this what you wanted?"

Tiny didn't give Amanda a chance to answer. "She's wearing the kimono. End of story."

I dropped my voice and said to Harper, "If you don't want to do this job, you better say so now and get your things. But I need to tell you, you won't be getting a positive referral from Amanda, and you might want to rethink your decision to get into modeling if this bothers you so much."

Tears spilled down Harper's cheeks and dripped onto the silver lamé. The drops rolled down the surface. I held out a box of tissues, and she pulled three out in quick succession. Up close, she looked even younger than I'd originally thought.

"Tell you what," Tiny said to Harper. "I'll look at it after I finish dealing with our shoe emergency." Tiny glared at me, her momentary expression of compassion instantly replaced with annoyance. "Apparently you had something to do with that too."

Harper blew her nose loudly and dabbed at her eyes. Tiny's response had done little to make Harper feel like she had been right to speak up. She'd treated her more like a robot than a human. The models—all of them—had been on their own since the day they'd first shown up. No one was looking out for these women.

Harper straightened up to her five-foot-nine-in-bare-feet height. "If Amanda wants me to wear the kimono, I'll wear the kimono, but only because Samantha stood up for me," she said to Tiny.

Tiny looked back and forth between the two of us and then walked away. Amanda went the other direction.

"I didn't stand up for you," I said to Harper. "I just asked the question."

"You went to Tiny. No one goes to Tiny."

I patted her arm in a soothing manner. "It's going to be okay. You have to admit she and Amanda seem to be leaving no room for error. That means they think you're going to rock that kimono better than anybody else here. Right?"

"I guess so." She sniffed twice in quick succession and blinked away more tears.

"I'll give you a couple of minutes to get it together. Amanda's having a meeting at quarter after six." I checked the wall clock. "That's in about ten minutes. Can you make it? I think it would be best if you're there and no one knows how you felt about this."

She blew her nose again. "I'll be there." Then her voice turned nasty. "I just wish Tiny wouldn't."

"You might be in luck. I think she's going out to get the shoes."

Harper looked up. "Mr. Taylor isn't coming here?"

"No."

"Oh. I like it when he comes. He makes everybody happy."

Now it was my turn for a tissue.

Harper left in the direction of the other models. She bent over her duffle bag and came up with a small makeup pouch. She pulled a bottle of eye drops and a compact from it and went to work on her red eyes and nose.

A flashbulb went off next to me. I blinked a couple of

times to make the black dots in front of my eyes go away. Someone with a camera had to be there, but the flash had temporarily blinded me. "Who are you and why are you taking my picture?" I asked.

"Clive Barrington." The dots faded, and I made out a silhouette of a man with his hand held out. I shook it. "Freelance photojournalist. Amanda agreed to let me document her show. I'm taking background shots tonight to flesh out the behind-the-scenes aspect."

Santangelo Toma had been right. This *was* turning into a circus.

Clive leaned against a cutting table. He was a moderately built man who I'd place in his forties. Longish golden blond hair was parted on the side and tucked behind his ears. His camera dangled from a black strap around his neck. He wore a T-shirt, plaid blazer, cuffed jeans, and green bucks. Those were nice. I wonder where you got a pair of green bucks these days? I was getting distracted. I looked back up at his face, and he winked at me.

"I think we might want to talk to Tiny about the pictures you're taking. I don't think she'd be too pleased with your presence here."

"Tiny left to get the shoes," Amanda said, having materialized from out of nowhere. "But Samantha's right. Maybe you've taken enough pictures for tonight."

Clive adjusted his lens. "A few more shots, and I'll be out of your hair."

"Keep it brief. The models don't need any more distractions."

"I'm going to sit in front of the runway." Clive turned to me. "Where are you going to be?"

"I can't see how that matters."

Amanda, who had started to walk away, stopped and turned back. "Samantha, maybe it's you who should leave."

I was tired and didn't mind the idea of going home and collapsing in bed. "What time should I be here tomorrow?"

"You don't need to come tomorrow. We've got it under control."

"But tomorrow is the show," I said.

"That's right. You can pick up your check at my studio on Monday." Amanda spoke with a finality that cut me to the quick. With one hand, she tossed her shiny black hair behind her shoulder.

I felt like I'd been stung center mass by a swarm of angry bumblebees. It was bad enough to have spent the past six weeks pushing aside petty jealousy to work with Amanda, but worse yet, she was firing me. If my back and knees and feet and shoulders didn't hurt so much, and if the caffeine from the pot of coffee I'd finished a few hours ago wasn't wearing off, then maybe I would have tried to establish my role backstage. But all things considered...

"Fine. I'll get my handbag and coat. Good luck," I said with as much dignity as I could muster. None of this had been easy. Nor appreciated, it seemed.

I weaved through the same labyrinth of rolling rods, mannequins, and fabric bolts that I'd worked around for the past few weeks and collected my belongings. I bundled up into a wool coat and hat and braced myself for the blast of cold from outside. Good riddance.

The main portion of Warehouse Five was connected to the front foyer and adjoining galleries of other artists by a hallway that ran the length of the building. I turned right and headed past the picked-over food service table toward the exit. Closer to the door, the lights were out. I flicked the switch on the wall next to the lavatories a few times, but nothing happened. *No worries,* I thought, as I trudged toward the glowing Exit sign.

And then I noticed a figure hovering in the parking lot. Fear folded around me like a blanket. *Act natural,* I coached myself. *Just keep walking. Your car is right outside the door.*

I fumbled for my keys, mentally kicking myself for not having them in hand already. The figure slunk back into the shadow. Adrenaline replaced the numbness of being dismissed, and the hair on the back of my neck stood up. I turned around to see if there was anybody else in the hallway with me. There wasn't. I pushed forward and then out the exit doors, with my head down. My car wasn't far.

And then a flicker of light caught my eye. I turned to look at the source, and quicker than you can say "supermodel," a trail of fire ignited a path from the edge of the parking lot to where I stood. I jumped away, too slowly. The flame licked my boot and climbed the hem of my pants. I swatted at my cuff, and the fire went out.

A figure in a puffy down coat stepped out of the shadows. I couldn't make out if it was a man or woman. He or she swung a lumpy bag that connected with my midsection, and I doubled over, my wool winter coat only absorbing some of the blow.

"Stay out of this," said a distorted voice. The person swung the bag again. I fell to the ground. My attacker ignited the bag with a match. The eerie orange light cast shadows over a face mostly hidden by a thick scarf.

The flaming bag struck me again and again. The ground

was cold through my coat, and I could barely move. The fire went out. I squeezed my eyes shut. Fabric tore, and round objects pelted me. I rolled to the side, my face wet with the tears of pain.

3

TRYING TO DISTRACT ME

"And that's where I found you," said Amanda from her seat next to the hospital bed. She wrung her hands as she spoke. She had just told us about finding me curled up in the parking lot, surrounded by burnt fruit, unable to stand or get help for myself. My memories of the previous evening had ended shortly after the beating stopped.

She'd done the right thing, calling 911 to get an ambulance for me and not letting anyone else into the area. When the EMTs arrived, I'd been taken to the hospital, where I relayed what little I could remember to a police officer after being poked, prodded, and X-rayed. My version had been told under the influence of painkillers and may have included a few extra details, but the overall gist was the same. I'd been attacked in the parking lot between the Warehouse Five exit and my car. I'd been beaten with a bag of oranges and set on fire. I'd been left to die or freeze, whichever came first. And now, thanks to Amanda, I lay recovering from internal bruising and second-degree burns.

My left hand was wrapped in a gauze bandage, and it hurt to take deep breaths.

"What time did you find her?" Eddie asked.

"It was a little after eleven. I went to the parking lot when some of the girls left. I wanted to see what was taking so long."

Eddie voiced my thoughts. "So nobody knows what happened."

"No."

I sat up and spoke in a raspy voice. "Somebody set me on fire and beat me. That's what happened."

"That's what you keep saying, but nobody saw anything. Tiny had to go meet Nick—" Amanda paused mid-sentence and looked at me. A tension-riddled silence ballooned into the small hospital room while every one of us wondered if I would react to the mention of Nick.

For the past six weeks, the name "Nick" had been a largely unspoken four-letter word. Our breakup had been unexpected; my ability to move on had been overestimated. The week I let it all sink in, I'd bought out the local grocery store's supply of frozen chicken tenders and subsisted on them, vanilla ice cream, and waffles for a week. I gained seven pounds, dropped out of society, and spent much of my time with my cat.

I love my cat, but there are some who might say my behavior was not entirely healthy. Still, there was no way I was going to let Amanda, Nick's maybe-former girlfriend, know how I felt.

Eddie took control of the conversation. "You said Tiny went out?" he asked.

"She went to pick up the samples at Nick's showroom. It seemed like a long time, but that's because we were at a standstill until she got back. I mean, there were little things for us to do like tack seams and steam samples and go over the order of the show, but I was keeping the models there so we could do a walk-through, and that cost us money. We couldn't do anything without the shoes."

"You were there late. The models were there late. Who else?" Eddie asked. In the background, the vital sign monitor beeped like the Atari videogame I'd gotten for Christmas in 1981.

"Interns and assistants, hair and makeup."

"What about other artists who rent space in the building?" Eddie pressed. In the past, it had been me asking the questions in circumstances like this. Tonight, I was happy to let Eddie step in while I listened.

"They were gone for the night."

"You're sure?"

"The last one to leave was an artist. He complained to Tiny about the noise before he left."

I strained to speak. "What about the photographer, Clive Barrington? Was he still there?" The effort of speaking made me cough.

Amanda averted her eyes. In that moment, I recognized the look. It wasn't guilt. It wasn't appreciation. It wasn't sympathy. It was pity.

"Clive, Amanda. Was he there?" I asked again, this time with more conviction.

"I don't know if he was there or not. He said he wanted to get a few pictures of the models walking the runway, but I don't think he knew we'd keep him waiting for hours."

"Who does he report to?" I asked.

"Nobody. He comes and goes as he pleases. When he started, he made a point of telling us he needed unlimited access if he was going to capture my story. Tiny agreed as long as she got picture approval before anybody else saw them. That was her demand. That we see the photos before any of them went public."

"Was there anyone else there that you remember?" Eddie asked Amanda. "Or you?" he asked me.

I watched Amanda, not knowing if she was going to return the eye contact. She didn't. She stared at her hands and fidgeted with her bracelet. If I hadn't noticed a slight movement at her temple, I might not have recognized that she was clenching and unclenching her teeth.

"I would have to think about it," I said. "Everyone I remember had a legitimate reason for being there. Do you agree, Amanda?"

She nodded her head. Something buzzed in her red crocodile handbag. We all watched as she fished it out and looked at the display. She hit a button that stopped the sound and tossed it back inside then looked up to find us all looking at her.

"It's not important," she said. Her handbag buzzed again. She ignored it, but the buzzing continued. After several buzzes, text message alerts, and vibrations, Eddie stated the obvious.

"Someone seems to disagree with you."

She stood and gathered her coat. "I need to get back to Warehouse Five. There's a lot to do before the show." She walked to the door and then stopped and turned back around. "I should have known something like this would happen." Then she left.

Breakup Rule #2: Don't be seen as a victim. I'd been hired to help Amanda at Nick's request, and I'd gotten attacked. It was her runway debut, her big show, her production. I'd only shown up that first day to honor my commitment and make sure nothing outside of positive things could be said about my character when she spoke to Nick about me. Now, I was unmade-up, with hospital hair, in paper pajamas. There was no way she could keep this story from him. Seeing as how I was at the center of the drama—through no fault of my own—there was a good chance Nick would see things the way Amanda would paint them: with me at the epicenter. I'd become an unanticipated inconvenience to her carefully scheduled timetables.

I waited for the door to shut and then turned to Eddie. "You have to get me out of here. It's going to take me longer than usual to get ready, but there's no way I'm going to miss her show."

"Are you nuts?" he asked.

"We both know I'm going to her show. We both know you're going to help me. Go get a nurse, and find out how I get out of here."

"Dude, you can try to talk me into helping you, and there's a chance you might be successful. That's why I'm leaving you here in the hands of the professionals."

"Eddie, I don't have insurance. I can't afford to get a bill for whatever they might do if they keep me here."

"You're not invincible. You were beat up with a bag of fruit. Who does that?"

"It was a warning. Like a scene from *The Grifters*." I hadn't given much thought to the choice of fruit as weapon. But in that movie, a bag of oranges had been used to beat up Angelica Houston because it caused internal injuries with minimal external bruising. I held my hands out and traced the burns on my left hand with the fingers on my right. "I don't get the fire, though. If somebody wanted to attack me without leaving evidence, why go with an open flame?"

"I know what you're doing," Eddie said. "You're trying to distract me with movie references and words like 'evidence.' It's not going to work. You're in a hospital bed, suffering from internal injuries and second-degree burns. For real. This isn't a movie. I know you like danger, but this is probably the safest place you can be."

"I don't like danger," I said.

Eddie raised one eyebrow. "I'm not going to help you get out of here before you're ready." He pulled on his bomber jacket and left.

There was a tap on my door, and a nurse entered. She took my blood pressure and asked if I needed anything.

"May I use the phone?"

She carried the old desk set to the table next to my bed. "Privacy?"

I nodded.

She left, and I called a number from memory. "Hello, Dante? It's Samantha Kidd. Are you free tonight?"

4

SMART, SAFE, AND SENSIBLE

Dante Lestes was a somewhat mysterious photographer from Philadelphia. I'd met him when a promotional contest in town inspired me to plan a heist. Dante had surprised me in the past by helping me when others wanted me to play it safe. He accepted that I ran head-on into impossible situations, and he'd given me the tools to protect myself. He had experience working for a private investigator, and while I was far from being a detective, I paid attention when he shared his knowledge with me. I might never be Kinsey Millhone, but I was a quick study.

Dante was everything Nick wasn't: dangerous, tattooed, and accepting of my lifestyle choices. In the past, he'd hinted that he was interested in getting to know me better. I, being of post-breakup mental fragility, hadn't followed up on those hints. But tonight, I figured a fashion show was a perfect place to set a new ball in motion. Keeping things on my turf, so to speak.

The tests at the hospital showed nothing that wouldn't heal in time. The doctor gave me the option of staying another night, an offer that came with pain medication and all the green Jell-O I could eat or going home. Even though it hurt to breathe, and some of my skin was blistered and red, I chose to leave. If I'd had insurance, I might have seen things differently, but that's the glamorous life of a fashion-industry professional with a recently spotty work history.

My plan wasn't completely foolproof, but I'd worked through the important issues. My car was still at Warehouse Five, but there wasn't time to retrieve it now. I took a taxi back to my house, filled Logan's bowl with cat chow, showered, and thought about how I would gain entry to the show. Having spent considerable time working there, I planned to talk my way past whoever was working the door. No way would Amanda have thought to ban me.

The shower, makeup, and hair-drying process kept me preoccupied, but by the time I had to choose an outfit, I had second thoughts about leaving the house. The local cable channel would broadcast the show. I'd already set up a recording. Maybe that would be the smart, safe, sensible thing to do.

I pulled on a loose-fitting black jersey trapeze dress, thigh-high stockings, and kitten-heeled boots. My ribs were still tender, and I didn't want to fuss with a waistband. I pulled my long hair up into a high ponytail and clipped a conical gold piece around the base of it then added gold hoop earrings and an arm filled with bangles. My injuries were hidden. Only I knew they were there.

Only I would know that someone had waited in the parking lot for me, lit me on fire, and pummeled me with a bag of fruit like a prison warning. I had to know why.

Screw smart, safe, and sensible.

By the time Dante arrived, I was ready. I opened the

door. Dante stood in front of me. His amber eyes locked onto mine then slowly traveled down to my lips then my body, where they lingered for a moment too long before he looked back into my eyes. I felt heat coming off him, heat coming off me. I held onto the door, taking shallow breaths, partly because it hurt to take bigger ones, and partially because being around Dante left me out of breath.

I guess being alone with Dante wasn't terribly smart, safe, or sensible either.

"So, we're going to your friend's fashion show, right?"

I didn't bother explaining the nuanced relationship between me and the designer-slash-maybe-former girlfriend of my ex and simply nodded.

Dante had traded his motorcycle for a late-seventies Corvette Stingray with orange flames. Not only were we going, but we were going to arrive in style.

I gave Dante directions to the warehouse district. It was in a stretch of five abandoned factories that had been bought out by a special interest group and subleased as gallery space to local artists. Quilters, painters, jewelry designers, and other creative types shared room in the converted building, occasionally banding together for open houses and community activities. Officially, the building was named after the investors, but locally they were referred to by the faded numbers that had long ago been painted on the exteriors. Warehouses one through four sat vacant.

Dante wasn't one to fill the air with chatter, but I'd learned that his silences didn't mean he was bored. There were times when I'd seen him in action, and I wondered if he had the same need for excitement that I did. I didn't ask. Tonight, I thought it best to keep him in the dark about my recent attack. I didn't want another lecture, and I certainly didn't want him to turn the car around.

The parking lot was close to full. Dante handed the car keys to a valet attendant. I got out of the car. A cold wind snapped at my face and ankles. I pulled my coat around me and caught the door that was being held open from inside. The person holding the door was Nick.

The last time Nick and I had been face to face had been six weeks ago, outside my house, discussing the merits/flaws of my personality. At the time, I'd been acting as his office manager by day and his girlfriend by night. A few days after that conversation, he'd reached the conclusion that my working for him wasn't a great idea. He replaced me with a recent college grad and suggested I work with Amanda.

Clearly, that had worked out well.

"Kidd," he said. His voice was soft and warm, like honey dissolving into a mug of hot tea. "I didn't expect to see you here tonight."

I hadn't expected to see him either, a fact made painfully clear by the reaction of my nervous system. I tipped my head to the side and pulled my ponytail over one shoulder. "Hi," I said.

Nick had thick, curly brown hair that he kept trimmed in a neat business-like style. He'd taken to wearing it differently. Longer and slightly unkempt, which gave him a boyish look. Instead of a shirt and tie like he normally wore for industry events, he was in a long-sleeved T-shirt, jeans, and Converse sneakers. He looked more like one of the interns running around backstage than a highly respected shoe designer.

"I heard about the attack. Are you okay?" he asked. Behind him, Amanda watched us. For as many times as I'd wondered how I'd react the next time I saw Nick, I'd never thought it would be twenty-four hours after being released from the hospital while his maybe-former girlfriend glared at us from twenty feet away. At least I was wearing lipstick.

We were a foot apart. He smelled like clean sheets and freshly baked doughnuts and New Year's Eve. I looked away from his root-beer-barrel-colored eyes to his T-shirt. A piece of lint clung to his sleeve. I picked it off. He reached out for my hand, but a shock of electricity sparked at his touch, and we both pulled away.

"Samantha?" Dante said behind me. I looked over my shoulder at him and then back at Nick.

The two eyed each other. When it seemed obvious I wasn't going to make an introduction, Dante held out his hand. "Dante Lestes," he said.

"Nick Taylor." They shook. Nick turned back to me. "You shouldn't be here. Not after what happened."

I didn't say anything, and the tension grew to an uncomfortable level. Someone opened the door next to us, and a gust of cold air entered. I stepped away from Nick. "Hope everything goes well tonight," I said. I left him in the hallway and followed Dante through the crowd.

The setup of the show wasn't all that different from other runway shows I'd attended. Rows of collapsible white chairs were set up on either side of a raised white platform. A screen occupied the end of the runway, and Amanda's name was mounted on it in large silver vinyl letters. Colorful lights cast an ethereal orange, red, and yellow glow across the audience. Large urns of orange roses sat on tall cocktail tables at the back of the room, and thousands of orange rose petals were strewn down the runway. Dante followed me as I weaved through the crowd, selecting two seats by the back. I didn't need to be in front. I didn't need to be noticed.

I looked for familiar faces. Buyers from Tradava, Ribbon's own department store where Eddie worked, sat in front-row seats along the right-hand side. As was the norm for a fashion show, a couple of pop stars were mixed into the crowd with an actress who was going to be starring in a new political drama. For a show two-plus hours west of New York, Amanda had drawn an impressive crowd.

Dante tipped his head closer to mine. "If I'd have known you were going to ignore me, I might not have accepted your invitation."

I blushed. "I'm sorry. I get distracted at these things, looking for people I know."

"Me too." He pointed to the end of the platform. "There's one."

I followed his finger and saw Clive snapping pictures of the crowd.

"You know Clive Barrington?"

Dante chuckled. "'Clive Barrington.' I never heard anybody use his full name before. We used to call him Bare. We competed for a few jobs, but Bare always had a taste for the ladies and eventually it got him into trouble."

"What trouble?"

"Underage girl at an unchaperoned photo shoot. Turned into a he-said-she-said thing. Nobody knows what happened, but he couldn't get a job after that. To tell you the truth, I didn't know he'd resurfaced."

"I wonder how he hooked up with Amanda?"

"Who knows? Looks pretty much the same as he did back then. A little older, a little less hair. The glamorous life is taking its toll on him. Back in the day, he wouldn't have been caught dead with highlights."

It had never occurred to me that Dante might know anyone at the show tonight. I watched him watch Clive and wondered what he was thinking. Before I had a chance to ask more questions, the lights went down.

Loud Japanese pop songs filled the air. A Godzilla movie was projected onto the back of the stage, above Amanda's name. A model walked out, dressed in a silver leather motorcycle jacket over a red pantsuit. Her hair was bright red at the roots, fading to orange then yellow, and cut in a bob with heavy bangs. She sauntered down the runway, posed at the end, then turned. Even from the back row I could make out the intricate red embroidery on the back of her jacket. The crowd applauded eagerly.

The next model started down the runway. She wore a black leather corset over a silver pantsuit. Her orange wig was pulled back into a chignon, secured with silver chopsticks.

The third girl stomped down the runway in a red Lycra halter dress. Her wig was yellow.

By the time the fifth model came out, it was clear that the audience was sitting up and taking notice of what Amanda was showing. Did it matter that her choice of venue was a downtown warehouse in Ribbon? Who was to say. More and more designers who had neither the money nor the connections to pull off a major event in New York City were orchestrating pop-up fashion shows, inviting as many industry insiders as they knew, and hoping for the best.

But this was not Amanda's first rodeo. She'd spent years interning for a famous designer before parting ways and taking a job with a local department store. On the side, she focused on her own collection, slowly building a name for herself by reinventing the classics. What I saw tonight was more than a slight departure from the styles that had originally gotten her noticed. But what was fashion without risk? And who ever said that a futuristic silver jumpsuit wouldn't one day be a classic?

A familiar figure stepped onto the stage. It was Harper, the reticent model in the ill-fitting kimono. Her silver wig was cut in a blunt bob like the first model. Her lips, painted tomato red, were shaped in a pout. The kimono still didn't fit, but tonight Harper showed she was the professional they'd wanted. Her sleeves hung down to the floor, making her look like a child playing dress up. She sashayed down the platform, hips swinging from side to side, creating the illusion of sex appeal even though I knew her to be mostly skin and bones. A trail of smoke followed her.

A smattering of applause filled the auditorium as if what we were watching was part of the show. But something wasn't right. A thin orange stripe appeared to hover just above the rose petals that scattered over the ground as Harper walked. First one then another of the rose petals ignited like small bursts of glowing light. And then a whole bunch of the petals caught fire in a path that followed Harper.

And then suddenly, her kimono erupted in flames.

5

MAKE-OUT POINT

THE HOUSE LIGHTS CAME ON. THE SUDDEN CHANGE OF illumination temporarily blinded me. Someone screamed. As my eyes adjusted, I followed the screaming to Harper. She fumbled with the sash on the kimono. Flames climbed the sleeves from the ground up and wrapped her like a special effect in a movie. She clawed at the fabric. Smoke filled the air, compromising visibility.

Nick appeared from behind the screen where Amanda's name was printed. He ran toward Harper and yanked the kimono from her shoulders. She left it in a burning pile and ran toward an exit. The flames caught onto the rest of the rose petals that covered the runway. More screams, now from the crowd. People stampeded toward the exits, bottlenecking the doorways with bodies trying to get outside. The fire grew, feeding off the fabric and oxygen in the room. I lost sight of Nick.

Dante tugged me the opposite direction of the crowd. "This way," he said.

I took his hand and barely kept up as we weaved past the frantic audience. We stumbled over flipped chairs and discarded drinks that now littered the floor. The fire had flashed over, climbing the walls and the ceiling. Sweat dripped from my hairline despite the cold night air. Within seconds, sprays of water shot out of the sprinkler system. We reached a set of double doors. He stepped back and pushed me through them.

We made it to the exit and fell outside. Fire trucks flooded the parking lot, sirens blaring. Professionals went to work on the fire. In the pandemonium, Dante took his keys from the valet booth. He scooped me up, one arm behind my head, the other under my knees, carried me to his car, and set me in the passenger seat. I closed my eyes while he drove us away from the scene. It wasn't until I heard the engine turn off that I opened them and saw that he hadn't taken me home.

We were parked in a vacant lot that overlooked a spectacular view of Ribbon. Lights from the streetlamps that illuminated the grid of downtown created a dense glow that slowly expanded into less and less, until it became the nothingness of the neighboring towns. In high school, we called this Make-Out Point.

"You want to tell me why your ex-boyfriend said you shouldn't have gone to the show?"

"He was worried about me, that's all."

"Does he have a reason to worry?"

I played with the gold bracelets on my wrist. "I had an incident yesterday."

"Samantha, don't beat around the bush with me."

"I've been helping Amanda with her show. Yesterday

there was a fire outside of Warehouse Five. I don't know how it started. It came right to me across the parking lot to where I stood, and I caught on fire. I dropped and rolled to put out the flames, and while I was down someone approached me. They were bundled up in an oversized coat, and from my spot on the ground, they looked humungous. They told me to stay out of it, but I don't know what 'it' is. And then they beat me with a sack of fruit and set me on fire."

"Fruit?"

"Oranges, tangelos, and clementines. When Amanda found me curled up in the parking lot, they were scattered around me."

"What happened after that?"

"I spent the night in the hospital."

"Why did you call me?"

I looked down at my hands. I didn't want to make eye contact when I said this part. "Everybody else told me to stay home. They thought it was too dangerous for me to come here tonight." I snuck a peek at his face but couldn't tell what he was thinking.

"Do you know who attacked you?" he asked.

"No."

"Someone involved with the show?"

"Maybe. I don't know."

"Are you in pain right now?"

"Yes."

He started up the car. "I'm taking you home."

"No. My car is still at the warehouse," I said. "Take me back there. Please." It had been too much activity for one day. My ribs ached, and I couldn't breathe. I needed to sit down, lie down, rest, sleep. My internal injuries throbbed, and even if the hospital had determined that none of them were serious, they hurt. Badly.

Dante reached for my handbag and found my prescription inside. He shook a tablet into his palm and handed it to me.

"You're in pain. Take this." He handed me a bottle of water from the cup holder.

I swallowed the pill and sank back against his bucket seats, trying to keep the seatbelt from digging into my midsection. The tension from the runway show, the medication for the pain, and the overall exhaustion of my life combined, and the world went dark as I fell asleep in the car.

Breakup Rule #3: Don't wake up in another man's bed. The bed was comfortable enough, but it wasn't mine. It took me a second to recognize whose bed it was. Dante's.

Dante lived in a studio apartment on Duryea Drive, on the side of a mountain off the beaten path of Ribbon. He'd once explained it as the place he kept here when not living in Philadelphia. I'd been here before but never on a sleepover.

Being a studio apartment, the interior wasn't divided up into separate rooms. It was one large room that split off to the right into a modest kitchen and to the left into a modest bathroom and makeshift closet. The bed that I currently occupied was of the futon variety. Which meant there wasn't any place else to sleep, which meant even though I was alone now, I probably hadn't been last night.

Not sure how I felt about that.

There was a tap on the front door, and then Dante entered. He carried a bag from the grocery store. I pulled the comforter up around me.

"You're awake," he said.

"I am."

"You want breakfast? Bacon? Eggs?"

"Sure." Things were getting curiouser and curiouser. But I was already slightly down the rabbit hole. Why not get some bacon while there?

I peeked under the sheet and saw that I'd slept in a T-shirt and sweatpants, neither of which were mine. I stood up and hopped across the cold hardwood floor to the bathroom. My dress, smelling faintly of wet ash, hung over the curtain rod. I found an empty hanger in Dante's closet and hung the dress up, did other bathroom-type things, and rejoined him.

The futon had been folded up, and a small table with a large plate of bacon and eggs sat on a table in front of it. There were forks poised on either side of the plate. Dante patted the seat next to him. Rocky and Bullwinkle filled the screen. I pinched a piece of bacon and ate it before sitting.

"You should have told me about the attack," he said.

I figured we'd get around to this sooner or later. "I don't always make the best decisions."

"That's a very mature thing to admit."

I shrugged. (I couldn't say anything else. My mouth was full.)

"I talked to my sister this morning," he said.

Dante's sister, Cat, traveled in the same fashion circles that I did. "How is Cat?"

"She's great. She's in Paris on a buying trip." He continued. "She filled me in on your recent history. Helps explain last night."

My initial antagonistic relationship with Cat had

morphed first into acquaintances and then into friendship. She knew about my employment issues since moving to Ribbon, about my frequent run-ins with the law, and about my recent breakup with Nick. If you needed gossip on me, she could give you the Cliff Notes version.

"I don't question the fact that you wanted to go to the show. Your ex and I have very different ideas on letting you live your life, regardless of what appears to be questionable judgment. But like I said, you should have told me."

"What did you expect me to say? 'Somebody put me in the hospital at a fashion show rehearsal, and now I need help figuring out who it was'? You were going to pretend that was normal?"

"You think asking me out on a date was normal?"

"What's so abnormal about that?"

"You were set on fire outside of the rehearsal, and there was a fire at the show last night. Somebody put a lot of people in jeopardy. If you hadn't been attacked, it might have seemed like an accident. But connect the two, and there's forethought. Somebody intended to hit that show. That same somebody thinks you're a threat."

It was true. Hearing him spell it out made it all the more real and scary. I couldn't pretend everything was okay. I set the bacon back on the plate.

"I keep trying to figure out what I know. Somebody attacked me. Me. Not anybody else connected to that show. All I've been doing for the past month is showing up at Warehouse Five to help Amanda get the show ready. I agreed to do it for reasons I don't want to get into. It was important to me to fulfill my obligation and protect my reputation. I didn't threaten anybody, I didn't see anything shady, and I didn't have any confrontations. I was the perfect employee. And if you must know, Amanda basically fired me before I was attacked."

"That may all be true, but somebody still set the show on fire. What else do you remember about what happened?"

"The warning. 'Stay out of it.' What is 'it?' How can I stay out of 'it' if I don't know what 'it' is?" I tried to stand but doubled over as a flash of pain shot through my torso.

"Slow down, Samantha. You might not be in the hospital anymore, but it's going to take time for you to heal. For now, you'll have to rely on me for whatever you need."

"I'm not moving in with you."

"Don't worry. It's temporary. And I'm not the babysitting type. Can you drive a motorcycle?"

"No."

He tossed me a set of keys. The key fob was shaped like a flame. "Looks like the Stingray is your ride for the next couple of days, but for the record, I think it's best that you stay away from the places you usually go."

"Why?"

"You don't know who attacked you or why. You might be able to explain it away as wrong place, wrong time, but I'm not a big believer in coincidence."

"You think someone might still be after me?"

He nodded once. The thought, now verbalized, was troubling. I wanted to discount his theory, but at my core, I agreed with him.

After breakfast was finished, Dante shrugged into his black leather jacket and left the house. As soon as his motorcycle disappeared around the curve of Duryea Drive, I tossed the dirty dishes in the sink and changed the channel to the local news. I'd expected the fire to be the top story. It wasn't.

In typical obsessed-with-celebrity nature, the top story was about how the rising star in the modeling world had been spotted on a plane that landed in Mexico last night.

Somehow, in the middle of all the chaos, Harper had managed to skip town.

6

GODZILLA ON THE MOON

GRAINY FOOTAGE OF HARPER STEPPING OFF A PLANE FILLED the screen. The clip was only a few seconds long and seemed to have been filmed from someone's cell phone. Harper's hair was pulled back into a ponytail, and she wore an oversized black topcoat and jeans. A duffle bag hung over one shoulder, the only luggage she appeared to have with her. She looked directly at the person filming her, hoisted the duffle bag strap higher, and hustled the other direction. The clip repeated as the reporter spoke.

"A vacationer headed to Cancun captured this footage after recognizing Harper Ashton when she boarded the plane. He said she arrived in full makeup but removed it during the flight. Ms. Ashton had left the ill-fated runway show of designer Amanda Ries. I believe we have a report on that show as well."

The footage switched to a view of Warehouse Five. An investigative reporter stood about a hundred feet in front of the now-abandoned warehouse. Fire had ravaged the building, leaving black stains on the outer edge of doorways and windows, like fake eyelashes that had clumped. The camera panned the exterior of the building.

"Last night a fire at Warehouse Five threatened to take the lives of many fashion insiders. The city of Ribbon has been offering tax incentives to local businesses, and Amanda Ries, local designer, had taken them up on that. Her runway show had been widely publicized from here to New York City, drawing buyers of major department stores who were eager to see this new collection. Touted as Godzilla on the Moon, Ries's show promised a departure from her early classic style. Only six looks walked the runway before an unexpected fire broke out, causing the warehouse to be evacuated. We have not been able to reach a representative from Amanda Ries's studio for comment."

I felt sick. The bacon churned in my stomach, and an acidic taste gurgled up into my throat. I filled a glass of water, chugged it, and then sat back down and clicked off the TV.

Only six looks had come down the runway. The sixth was Harper's kimono. There had been something off about that garment from the start. The poor fit, the assignation to Harper, and the refusal to alter it. The rest of the show had gone off as fashion shows do. Which made me think that someone had planned all along to use the kimono to start the fire.

Was that why I'd been attacked? Because someone didn't like the fact that I spoke up on behalf of Harper and asked for it to be altered? Because maybe someone had been planning all along to sabotage the show, and the kimono had been the trigger?

But rigging a garment to ignite on the runway in the middle of a show was a pretty out-there concept. I couldn't help thinking how many people had a stake in a fashion show's success: designer, financial backer, models, model management, venue, press. And every single one of these people had not only been there but had access. Would one of them gain more by destroying the show than helping to create it? What secret had been hidden amongst the garments and the shoes and the rose petals?

This wasn't the first disastrous runway show in fashion history. The year Lindsay Lohan was affiliated with Ungaro and failed to appear was bad. So was an early Michael Kors show when plaster fell from the ceiling of the loft where the show took place and landed on the heads of some high-profile models. But neither was this bad. A collection that quite literally went up in flames.

Amanda wasn't the luckiest of designers. A little over a year ago, she'd been favored to win a local design competition that never took place because one of the judges was killed. While she missed out on the cash prize, the publicity helped her land financial backers who funded her debut runway collection tonight. But like I said, luck wasn't on her side. People knew her name but little more. There might be no such thing as bad press, but for a designer, sooner or later you've got to prove your worth. Otherwise you're little more than a runner-up on a canceled reality show. No one quite remembers who you are.

It didn't take long for me to find out what everyone was talking about even though I was squirreled away at Dante's house. The local news, the internet, and the *Ribbon Times* fed me information. None of which compared to what I could find out from Eddie. I found my phone sitting on an end table and called him.

"Hey, dude," he said. "How are you feeling?"

"A little banged up but mostly okay."

"You heard about Amanda's show?"

I paused for a second, weighing the pros and cons of admitting that I'd ignored his cautionary words and had gone to Warehouse Five anyway. "I heard," I said.

"It was crazy, dude. People went nuts. I didn't think I was going to get out of there alive."

"You were there?"

"Tradava arranged for me to attend. I got there right when the lights went down."

Tradava was the reason I'd left my job as Senior Buyer for designer shoes at Bentley's New York. Well, maybe the chance to start over was the reason, but Tradava was the enabler. I wouldn't have quit my job in New York without something lined up in Ribbon, and when I'd landed that job, I'd felt the planets aligning to give me a chance to get on the road less traveled. It was either my greatest spontaneous decision or my greatest mistake; the jury was still out on which.

After landing the trend specialist job at Tradava, the fashion director who hired me was murdered, and everything went downhill from there. A year into my relocated life in Ribbon, I didn't know if I wanted to work for a company who had shown little (no) interest in employing me once the murder was cleared up. Still, they had benefits.

"Do you think you could do me a favor?" I asked.

"Sure. Are you still at the hospital? Need me to sneak in a meatball sandwich?"

"No. I—I went to the show last night too. With Dante. And now I'm at his apartment. Can you swing by my house and check on Logan?"

"I'm not sure which part of that to comment on first. You went home with Dante?"

"Yes, but it's not like that."

"I'm reminded of a phrase that includes frying pans and fires, but in light of what happened last night, to say it out loud might be in poor taste. Let's just say I hope you know what you're doing," he said. "And yes, I'll check on your cat on my lunch break."

"Thank you," I said. Tires crunched in the driveway out front. I peeked out the window. Dante's motorcycle pulled onto the bottom of the gravel-covered driveway and slowly snaked up to the house. "I'll call you back," I said and hung up.

I opened and shut a few drawers in Dante's kitchen, looking for a scrap of paper and a pen. I needed to take notes of what I remembered from Warehouse Five last night while the memories were still fresh. At home, I knew where I kept everything. In Dante's apartment, I was at a loss.

The third drawer down was filled with an assortment of cards and photos. And the photo on the top was of Dante, a pretty blonde, and a young boy. I flipped the photo over. In green pen was the caption "Dante, Linda, and Jameson."

I should stop. I knew I should stop. I should put the photo back in the drawer, close the drawer, take a Sharpie out of one of the cups next to sofa and write my notes on a napkin. But instead, I pulled out the next several photos. The blonde and the boy by a birthday cake. Jameson's 6th birthday. And one of Dante and the boy fishing. Happiness —and similar bone structure—evident in both of their faces.

The click of the door hijacked my attention, and the photo floated to the floor.

"I forgot my wallet," Dante said from the doorway.

"I was looking for a piece of paper," I said.

"Paper's in the bottom drawer."

"I didn't get to that one yet."

He walked over and scooped the photo from the floor. The open drawer was next to my thigh. He dropped the photo into the drawer and pushed it closed with his knee. I didn't move. When he stood, he was inches away from me.

"I have a son. He's seven now. He and his mom live in Philly."

I tried to act nonchalant, to pretend I wasn't curious or surprised, but I felt the heat climb my face and suspected that I was failing miserably. "I thought when you weren't here, you lived in Philly."

"I do."

"You're not married, are you?"

"No."

"Were you?"

"She and I didn't work. It's about what's best for Jameson."

"Do you see him often?"

"Weekends, mostly."

"But today is a weekend, and you're here."

"Something else came up."

I looked away, embarrassed. I was suddenly overwhelmed with questions that I had no right to ask.

"I'm sorry about the violation of your privacy," I said.

"No worries." He stepped away from me and glanced down at my T-shirt. I crossed my arms over my chest. He smiled. "How's the pain?"

"I'll deal. It'll get better."

"In time. With rest."

"And what happens in the meantime? Whoever did this gets away with it?"

"Gets away with what?" Dante prodded.

"I don't know."

"I've been thinking about it myself."

"And?"

"And I haven't reached any conclusions. You look like you have a couple of theories. Use me," he said, and cocked an eyebrow, "as a sounding board. Unless you want to use me for something else."

"We are not going to have that conversation while I have an assortment of internal injuries around my midsection."

"That's fair." He did a poor job of stifling a grin.

As much as Dante knew from his work with a private investigator, this wasn't his world. It was mine. And I could use a fresh perspective.

Ever since moving to Ribbon, I'd surrounded myself with people who knew what the fashion world was like. Nick was a shoe designer. Eddie was the visual director at Tradava. Cat owned an off-price designer boutique. Every one of us accepted the peculiarities of the industry as if they were normal. But here we were, with a sabotaged fashion show in our own backyard. Nothing normal about that. There was a possibility that Dante would listen to me, that he'd help me see something I hadn't seen so far.

Or there was the possibility that he was playing with me the way Logan played with the occasional chipmunk he caught in the yard. Swat them, let them run a few steps away, then catch them and swat at them again. I saw what Logan's game did to the chipmunks. I didn't want that to happen to me.

Dante turned on the sink water and washed the dishes.

He transferred them to a drying rack that sat on his counter. "I can tell you're wrestling with something," he said. "Let me know when you want to talk."

I bit my lip and stared at the coffee table. I still had too many questions I needed to work out.

"I'm going to take a shower," I said.

"Go crazy."

When I was done, I spritzed last night's dress with Dante's cologne and put it back on. I dried my hair, pulled it into a low ponytail, and then capped it with a gray houndstooth fedora from the Justin Timberlake part of Dante's closet.

When I returned to the living room, Dante was on the sofa, inspecting a camera and a couple of lenses on the table in front of him. "Is that my hat?"

"It is."

"Looks good on you."

"Thanks." I scooped up the keys, pulled on my black wool coat, and headed to the front door.

"Where are you going?"

"Out." I paused by the door, not sure if he was going to tell me when to be back, or if I was going to tell him where I was headed. A few seconds passed, and I left.

I have never driven a sports car before in my life. The concept of being handed the keys to a Corvette Stingray, no strings attached, was slightly beyond my grasp. I sat in the soft leather bucket seat and ran my hands over the steering wheel several times before starting the car. The engine roared to life the way the lion roars at the beginning and end of MGM movies. I undid the parking break, put the car in gear, and coasted down the driveway. I pulled onto Duryea Drive and followed the winding road until eventually I made it out to the streets of downtown Ribbon. Minutes later, I parked in front of Amanda Ries's workroom.

What was I doing here? I wasn't sure. What I was sure of was that Amanda did not want to see me or talk to me. After the way she'd dismissed me the night before the show, and after her reaction to me at the hospital, it had been clear that we weren't destined to become friends who braid each other's hair. But I'd been attacked because of my affiliation with her. Maybe nobody else was trying to find out who had assaulted me, but I wasn't willing to let it go.

I got out of the car and locked the doors then followed the sidewalk up to the front entrance. I paused in front of the white front door and tried on greetings and explanations as to why I was there. Much like bathing-suit shopping after the holidays, none of them fit. Before I came up with the perfect salutation, the front door opened inward. Tiny stood in front of me, barely contained in the frame of the door.

"Don't just stand there," she said. "Come on in. We've been expecting you since last night."

7

AN UNATTRACTIVE SHADE OF GREEN

I STEPPED BACKWARD AND GLANCED AT THE SIGN MOUNTED TO the left of the front door. "ARS | Amanda Ries Studios," it read. I tried to look around Tiny but was unsuccessful.

"What do you mean you've been expecting me? Nobody knew I was coming here." *I* didn't even know I was coming here. "Who is 'we'?"

"Your reputation precedes you. Amanda knew you'd show up sooner or later." She handed the door to me and headed inside. She turned around again. "Coffee?" she asked.

"Sure."

She went into the next room. I unbuttoned my coat but left it on. The only time I'd been here before, Amanda hadn't invited me inside. She'd met me at the front door with a rolling rack of garment bags filled with samples and closed the door behind me.

This time I was inside and more than a little curious. I couldn't say what it was about Amanda that got to me, unless I did a little soul searching and acknowledged a basal jealousy that left me feeling an unattractive shade of green.

Amanda had attended I-FAD, the Institute of Fashion, Art, and Design, with Nick. I didn't know how much intimacy was included in their college history, but they had remained close long after graduation. Amanda was gorgeous, with sleek, long black hair parted on the side, her perfect size-four figure, her five-foot-nine frame in flats, though she rarely wore them. She could have been one of the models walking the runway like Harper instead of the designer producing the clothes, and the fact that she'd chosen the more creative of the two paths, and showed every indication of being successful at it, seemed an unfair bounty of talent. At least, that's what a petty person would think. I was doing my best not to be petty. For now.

Amanda's waiting area was a study in black and white. The carpet was black and ran wall-to-wall. The walls were a crisp contrast. Abstract paintings on unframed canvases filled the walls. A vintage bust form, covered in black patent leather, sat by the front window, as if to welcome visitors with its limbless figure.

"Here's your coffee," Tiny said. "Cream, no sugar. Right?"

"Right. How'd you know?"

"I watched you make it every day for the past six weeks."

I wondered what else Tiny might have noticed about me in those weeks. Did she think I'd seen something I shouldn't have seen? Did she have reason to want to scare me off? Tiny might have been over six feet tall, but that didn't mean she was above suspicion. I took the mug from her outstretched hand and blew on the hot liquid.

"Sam, before Amanda comes out here, I want to say something. We both appreciate the work you did on the show. Neither one of us considers you in any way responsible. I don't know if that was ever made clear."

"Responsible for what?"

"Your little stunt brought on some bad publicity. The day before the show, claiming to have been attacked in the parking lot."

"I was attacked."

Tiny held up her hands, palm-side out. "I guess we'll never know the truth, will we?" She crossed her arms over her gray sweater. The cuffs on her white oxford had been unbuttoned and folded back, exposing a black utilitarian sports watch. Whatever jovial vibe she'd started out with had been replaced. "Like I said, Amanda and I expected you to show up. What's your take on the fire?"

"Somebody sent me to the hospital the night before the show. I don't know who, and I don't know why. A day later, a fire at the warehouse destroyed Amanda's show. I don't believe that fire was an accident. When I was attacked, I was warned to 'stay out of it.' The only business I've been involved with for the past six weeks is Amanda's business."

"You'd do well to walk away from the whole thing," Tiny said.

"You said my reputation preceded me. That means you know I'm not going to leave this alone."

"I don't get people like you," she said, shaking her head. "You make things far more complicated than they need to be. Nobody's asking you to be a hero. Why not just get on with your life?"

It was in high school that I first learned that people don't expect you to take the hard way. I was on the track-and-field team. Before each meet, our coach would gather us in the gymnasium and call out the different events. If we planned to compete in one, we called out our last name and he wrote us in.

I was one of six girls who had been tagged long-distance runners. There were only two events for us: half mile and mile. Nobody wanted to run the mile. Ever. But one day I decided I would. Coach called out "mile," and I called out "Kidd." He looked up from his clipboard and held my expression for a few seconds. I shrugged in a "why not?" gesture. He smiled and wrote down my name. From that day on, I ran the mile every time we had a competition.

If I was going to do something, I was going to go the distance.

"Tiny, I'm not going to let this go until I have answers."

"If you won't walk away for yourself, then walk away for Amanda."

It was at that moment that Amanda appeared from the kitchen. "Tiny, you're wrong. If anybody can help me, it's Samantha."

"You're making a big mistake," Tiny said. She grabbed a cross-body nylon bag that was propped along the wall and stormed out the front door without a coat. I watched through the front window as she hunched her shoulders against the wind and climbed into a black SUV then drove away.

Amanda lowered herself into a leather chair behind her large glass-topped desk. A vase filled with orange roses like the ones at her runway show sat on the corner. She held out a white business-sized envelope. "This is probably what you came here for. Your check. Take it. You earned it."

I took the envelope, folded it in half, and tucked it into my handbag. "Amanda, I didn't have anything to do with the fire," I said. "But I'm not going to forget that somebody jumped me."

She stared at me with a sort of curiously distaste, like a first-timer to Paris when presented with frog legs. "I don't know who attacked you," she said. "But you must know something I don't. Something that will help me figure out what's going on."

"The way Tiny just stormed out of here. Was that normal?" I asked.

"What's normal these days? I found you barely conscious in the parking lot outside of Warehouse Five. Twenty-four hours later my show went up in flames. It's hard to believe the two aren't connected. Tiny's convinced you had something to do with the fire. When you pulled up out front, she wanted me to call the cops."

"What possible reason could I have for wanting to make myself look like a victim and then burn down your show?"

Amanda opened a different drawer and pulled out a tri-folded piece of paper. "Maybe you should take a look at this."

She held the paper between her first two fingers the way Mae West would have held up an unlit cigarette. I took the paper and unfolded it. In mismatched letters that looked like they'd been cut from magazines, glued to the page, and then run through a copier, the paper said:

AMANDA RIES: BURN, BABY, BURN!

8

REMARKABLY NORMAL

I sank into one of the chairs across from Amanda's desk. "When did you get this?" I asked.

"The first one came about a month ago."

"There are more?"

Amanda dropped her eyes to the glass desktop. She pulled her sleeve over her hand and wiped in circles at a ring from a mug that hadn't been set on a coaster. When she finished, she pulled the bottom drawer of her desk open and pulled out a small stack of white papers bound with a yellow rubber band. When she looked at me again, her face was the picture of worry.

"So far there are six."

"May I?" I asked.

She nodded, and I took the pile. After pulling the rubber band off, I flipped through the pages. Each one held a threat spelled out in mismatched letters like the first. I ran my finger over the smooth paper. I couldn't picture Fonts.com having an option that looked like a pre-technology cut-and-paste blackmail note. Whoever had painstakingly assembled these pages of threats had access to fashion magazines and a lot of time on their hands. Whoever had done this was making a point. I doubted it was coincidental that fashion was Amanda's business.

"Take them. I don't want to look at them anymore," she said.

"Does Tiny know about the letters?" I asked.

"No."

"Do the cops?"

"Whatever you might think of me, you need to know one thing. I am remarkably normal. When I get a cold, I go to the doctor. When I drive through a shady part of town, I lock the doors and roll up the windows. And if I receive threats that look like the work of someone with a screw loose, I go to the police. I don't share your attraction to danger."

"I wish people would stop saying that."

"It's true. You get off on the thrill in a way I don't understand."

I stood up and pushed my sleeves back so she could see the burn marks on my wrists. "Do you see this?" I asked. "This would never have happened if I wasn't at your dress rehearsal helping you with your runway show. It never would have happened if you weren't trying to get me to leave. I'm not here because I get off on the thrill of being hospitalized for doing you a favor. I'm here because I don't want the person who did this to me to get away with it."

"Samantha, I never dreamed you would get hurt. Of all people, you. The day before the show gets sabotaged too. If you would have stayed in the hospital, you wouldn't even have been there."

"What are you saying, Amanda? You don't believe me, do you?"

She leaned back and crossed her arms. "Why did you agree to work for me? I might have understood if you and Nick were still dating, but you broke up. Nobody would have judged you if you'd said no, considering the circumstances."

"You know that's not true. Everyone would have judged me. Including you. If I hadn't shown up to help you after I said I would, you would have talked trash about me. And despite what you may or may not have heard, I have integrity. I know the fashion industry and was prepared to help you. And I did. End of story."

"A lot of people think the only reason you showed up was because you wanted to use me to get Nick back."

"If I were trying to get him back, the last place I'd be is here. Nick doesn't support my need to find answers."

"That doesn't affect you, does it? That he worries about you and the decisions you make?"

"I'm worried about the fact that I was attacked two nights ago. That's what I worry about."

Amanda dropped her eyes to the desk. She was hiding something. Did she know more about my attack but didn't want to tell me?

I pressed on. "There's an artist who rents space at Warehouse Five. He's been trying to get you banned from the building."

"Santangelo Toma. Tiny told me she'd take care of him."

"Take care of him how?"

"The same way she appeased the rest of the tenants. She offered them comp tickets to the show. Most of them were happy to accept."

"And Santangelo?"

"He tore up the tickets and threw them at her."

There was something hinky about Santangelo's behavior. I could understand him not being happy about the chaos Amanda and company brought to his studio space, but his animosity seemed disproportionate to the situation.

Before I could ask any more questions, a car pulled into the front driveway. I turned around and followed Amanda's stare out the picture window. The tall black man who'd been working with the models the night I was attacked got out of a midnight-blue BMW. He slammed the door and walked to the Corvette. He stopped by the driver's side window and bent down to peer inside.

"He was backstage on Friday night. Who is he?" I asked.

"Oscar LeVay. He owns OLV model management. Tiny worked with him to cast the show."

"Which means he was there the night of the show too?"

"Yes. He's been there every night this week."

I couldn't tell if Amanda was thinking what I was thinking, but the word "opportunity" was flashing through my brain like it was the name of a new show in Vegas.

"Were you expecting him?"

"No."

"Then I want to stick around and hear what he has to say. Where can I hide?"

The doorbell rang. Before she made a move toward it, she reached out and put her hand on my forearm. "You can't tell anybody about this conversation." There was open desperation in her voice.

We stood two feet apart, eyes locked in a face-off where lines were drawn and crossed. If this had been a western, there would have been tumbleweed and the cry of a coyote.

"Done," I said. I scanned the interior of her studio and noticed a hinged wicker screen that partitioned off the corner of the studio by a rolling rack. "What's behind the screen?"

"Nothing. That's where models change when there's mixed company."

I moved to the corner and stepped behind the screen. "Let that guy in, and pretend I'm not here."

"Why?"

"Just do it."

I ducked behind the screen and wedged myself onto the floor behind a round wicker hamper. I hadn't noticed if the lighting created a telltale shadow that would give away my presence, but I figured it couldn't hurt to be as indiscreet as possible.

I heard Amanda open the door. "Oscar, hi. Tiny just left. Is there something I can help you with?"

Heavy footsteps marched into the room. The door closed. I pictured the well-appointed man in the room with Amanda and wondered how she could possibly hold her own against someone as imposing as him.

"Amanda, I took a chance by hiring out Harper to your show and look what happened. She was my top girl. Now she's fled the country. Do you know what this will do to my business? She's been with me since she was fourteen. I've spent years grooming her for the big time. Every day I face a firing squad of mothers who are afraid to trust their girls to me, and I've built my fortune on being able to maintain the safety of every model in my charge. I've lost that reputation because of you."

"Oscar, my collection was ruined. *My* reputation took a hit, not yours."

"And your name is in every news outlet from here to Manhattan. Publicity stunts only work once, my dear. I don't care what circumstances there were, I expect you to pay in full." His voice grew louder, and I imagined the effect his words and attitude had on Amanda. I wished I could see, but there was no way to do so without giving myself away.

Or was there?

Amanda had a large mirror hanging on the outside of the powder room, and the door was partially open because the room was vacant. I strained my neck until I picked up the reflection of the two of them in the middle of the room.

Oscar was a good six inches taller than Amanda. An ivory pashmina scarf was draped around his neck and tucked into the front of his coat. He held a tweed hat, shifting it from one hand to the other.

"Oscar, be reasonable. Tiny manages the billing."

"I don't trust her. She's been nickel and diming me over the models' fees since we started casting this show. You had twenty of my girls. They get two fifty an hour with a minimum five-hour booking per day. That's twenty-five grand for the fittings, twenty-five grand for the rehearsal, and twenty-five grand for the show."

Seventy-five thousand for models for the runway show? I knew the fashion industry was lucrative for lots of parties involved but not in towns like Ribbon. I didn't believe Tiny would have agreed to those rates and not renegotiated the event as a total. Unless Tiny was getting a kickback on the side from the arrangement. Regardless of the models' height, I had a feeling they were getting short shrift.

Oscar continued to rant. Even from a short distance I could see a gloss of sweat beading on his shiny forehead. "I should sue you for the damage you've done to my business.

Harper was booked for the next year, and I'm going to lose those commissions."

Amanda's face went whiter than it had been. "Oscar, please calm down. I'll talk to Tiny when she returns, and I'll have her call you to discuss the situation."

"When will that be?"

"This afternoon."

"If I don't hear from her by three, I'm starting legal action against your company."

"That won't be necessary."

The doorbell rang. I couldn't see who had arrived, but I assumed if it was Tiny, she wouldn't have rung the bell.

"Excuse me," Amanda said. She disappeared from my sight.

Oscar moved closer to her desk. I ducked back, behind the screen, and held my breath. Had I left evidence of my presence behind? No. But there was one thing that I knew had been left on Amanda's desk: the threatening letters that she'd been mailed.

Maybe Oscar wouldn't see them. Maybe they'd be lost among the piles of invoices and sketches and notes scattered on the surface. "Oscar, I have to cut your visit short," Amanda said. "My lunch date is here."

"Tell Tiny I expect to be paid by the end of the week."

Footsteps sounded across the floor, and then the front door opened and shut. I stood up and stepped out from behind the screen.

The letters were missing.

9

A JOKE AT MY EXPENSE

"Samantha, get back behind the screen. Now," Amanda whispered urgently. Something about her tone told me to act first and ask questions later. The door opened again, and before I could twist around and look in the mirror to see who had arrived, she spoke in a falsely bright, unexpectedly loud voice. "Nick, you're early for lunch. Let me get my things. Bye, Oscar!"

Amanda had said nothing about Nick being on his way.

This was bad. No, this was beyond bad. Wearing the clothes I'd worn last night, now scented with Dante's cologne, I might be sending signals that could be misinterpreted. I also realized that hiding in Amanda's studio, discussing the threat on her company, could be considered me seeking danger. This wasn't the time or the place for me to debate the merits of my personality. Even my signals were sending signals.

Amanda knew I was hiding behind the screen. I doubted she'd out me. I ducked further into the corner and slouched behind the hamper. I didn't need to see anything else. What I needed was an invisible cape.

The door shut. "Were we planning on lunch? I don't remember that," Nick said.

"Oscar was here to meet with Tiny, but she went out. I didn't want him to stay indefinitely, so I said that for his benefit. Have you already eaten?"

"We're actually going to lunch?"

"I think it'll look bad if we don't leave. I mean, we said we were going out. If he's watching, he'll expect us to leave. We should. Leave. We should leave so we don't look suspicious."

For the briefest moment, I was proud of Amanda. She was right. I didn't know what to make of Oscar's tirade, and I didn't yet know how he fit into the bigger picture, but she was thinking like I would have thought. Good for you, Amanda.

Nick didn't say anything at first, and I had to fight every impulse to lean forward to see his expression. "Sure, okay. You're right. Let's get some lunch."

"What's wrong? You're acting like I said something funny."

"Your reasoning reminded me of someone else." He paused. "That's the first time that ever happened."

"Do I want to know who?" Amanda asked.

"Probably not."

I gave them a ten-minute lead and then left out the back door. I stood by the side of the building until Nick's truck pulled out of the driveway, then I snuck to the Corvette and left.

While I drove, my mind wandered back to Oscar's insensitivity. He'd been more concerned about money than the wellbeing of his clients. Now I had four people I didn't trust: Tiny, Clive, Santangelo, and Oscar. It would have been easy for any of them to set both fires, the one that ignited me and the one that destroyed Amanda.

My mind wandered back to the threats Amanda had received. Had Oscar pocketed them? It was curious that she'd even shown them to me, but it was also painfully clear that she had unspoken reasons not to trust anybody else. I needed to find out more about everybody who had access to Amanda's show.

Without putting much thought into it, I ended up at Warehouse Five.

Amanda had negotiated use of several adjoining rooms and the main hall for the runway show. I wondered how many people had been put out of business thanks to the fire, and how favorably she'd be viewed for upcoming events. It was odd that Santangelo appeared to be more upset than the rest of the artists who used space at the warehouse to showcase their creations. I wondered if there was something else behind the resentment he'd shown toward Amanda.

I parked at the far end of the lot and approached the building. The recent cold weather had long ago killed any plant life that had grown around the perimeter of the building, leaving only loose pebbles and broken chunks of concrete scattered on top of the macadam. Yellow caution tape had been wound around rusted-out poles that marked the edges of the lot. The tape had broken, and two ends now snapped in the wind.

The first set of doors I tried was locked, as was the second. By the third, I concluded that the building hadn't reopened after the fire. I pressed my face up to the glass and squinted, trying to make out the interior. A bright pop of a flash bulb blinded me. I stood up straight and blinked several times, waiting for the dots in front of my eyes to clear. The door to the building opened, and Clive Barrington leaned out.

"Just don't stand there. Come in, if you're coming in."

"What are you doing here?" I asked. "As far as I can tell the building is locked up."

"Documenting the aftermath," he said, tapping his camera. "'Model Sizzles On and Off Runway,'" he said. "Or maybe 'Designer Turns Up the Heat.' My contract gave me access to a much bigger story than documenting her twee show."

"Amanda knows what you have in mind?"

"I have unrestricted access and the freedom to do what I choose with the footage."

"I can't imagine anybody was happy about giving you access to come back today."

"Happy, no. I can't say they were either," Clive said with a grin.

"But yet, here you are."

"I can go anywhere Amanda went on one condition."

"What's that?"

"I turn over a copy of my photos to my new friend."

"Anybody I know?" I asked. Clive tipped his head toward a man who stood by the end of the building.

He was tall and thin and wore a tan sport coat over a white shirt and brown sweater. A brown, gray, and camel wool scarf was wrapped around his neck, and a camel tweed cap covered his head. The sleeves on his jacket were too short, as were the hems on his pants. Ichabod Crane came to mind. He stared at the windows of the building for a few seconds and then spoke into his phone.

"Who's he?"

"Arson investigator. He came with the cop."

That's when a second man stepped into view. Detective Loncar.

The detective appeared not to notice me at first, odd considering I'd been on his radar almost since the first day I arrived in Ribbon. Loncar and I had a history established through a couple of homicides. During at least one investigation, he'd filed me in the Person of Interest column. Considering my recent turn as victim, I thought the best tack was to let bygones be bygones and say hello. I excused myself from Clive and started across the loose gravel parking lot, wishing I had more practical shoes than the kitten-heeled boots I'd worn last night.

"Ms. Kidd. Why am I not surprised to see you here?" Loncar said before I reached him.

"Nice to see you, too, Detective," I called out. I walked past two orange cones and stepped over a white concrete beam that marked off a parking space. Loncar stayed where he was, looking at the exterior of the building. Unlike the arson investigator, Loncar wore a coat over his suit. The shoulders of his coat extended beyond his own shoulder line and sloped down above his arms. The cuffs of his pants broke across the front of his rubber-soled shoes. Considering his thick midsection, I would have suggested he avoid cuffs in the future, but he didn't appear to be in the mood for unsolicited fashion advice.

The arson investigator stepped forward and put his arms out on either side of him. "This is a restricted area. No access for the public."

Loncar turned to him. "It's okay," he said. "I got this

one." He bowed slightly and held his hand out toward the parking lot. "Lead the way, Ms. Kidd."

I looked at the lot and back at him then carefully stepped over the loose gravel in my heels. When I reached the macadam, I turned to face the detective. "Do you have any leads?"

He didn't answer right away. Instead, he turned and looked at the building, then at the arson investigator, and Clive.

"What brings you here?" he asked when he finally turned his attention back to me.

"The fire. I was here when it happened. I thought I'd come back, look around, see if anything stood out to me as being off."

He crossed his arms. "Ms. Kidd, perhaps you'd like me to sponsor your application to the police academy?" Before I could answer, he continued. "Because otherwise I can't figure out why you keep showing up at my crime scenes."

It seemed we'd furthered our relationship. Detective Loncar made a joke at my expense.

"Detective, you should talk to me about this. I could help you."

"Ms. Kidd, we've been over this. The city of Ribbon employs me to perform a job. If you want to join my team, feel free to go through the proper channels. Otherwise, it's best if you learn that I'm not going to share information with you."

I glared at him for a few seconds and then walked away. He could certainly point out that he wasn't going to tell me anything, but to ignore my attack and the possible connection to the fire was a new level of cold. If he wasn't going to help me find answers, I was going to find them myself.

I approached Clive, who had continued to take pictures while I was gone.

"How much is Amanda paying you?" I asked.

"We worked out a special rate." He smiled with half of his mouth and glanced down at my body, as if he were implying that the exchange involved something other than money. "I could work out the same rate for you if you're interested."

I wouldn't have minded learning some dirt about Amanda but considering how high Clive rated on my Sleaze-O-Meter, I could hardly believe what he was insinuating.

"Is there any way I could get a copy of your film too?" I asked.

"Not bloody likely. I'm afraid that's not in my power to negotiate. Hello, Inspector Gigger," he finished.

I turned to my left. The arson investigator had approached when I wasn't looking and now stood by my elbow. Loncar stood to his side and didn't look happy. Not that he usually exuded sunshine and daisies, but today, his attitude was more gutters and weeds than usual.

Ichabod Crane spoke up. "Mr. Barrington, I don't know what you're discussing with this woman, but I think it's important to point out that the photos you're taking are part of my arson investigation and are no longer your property."

"I can appreciate your position, Inspector. I'd rather give my film to you than to her any day. But I am a bit baffled as to why you don't want to talk to her."

"Why would we want to talk to her?"

"She's had as much access to the scene as I have."

Inspector Gigger looked at me with new interest. Clive pointed his camera at the building and the shutter clicked several times.

"He's right," I said. "I'm Samantha Kidd. Detective Loncar knows me. I've been working with Amanda Ries on her runway show. And before you think I had something to do with the fire, let me assure you, my only interest is in finding out who attacked me the night before the show."

Loncar scratched his head. "You were attacked, here, two nights ago?"

"Yes."

"If I go back to the station, will I find a police report?"

"Yes."

Clive stepped closer. "Go ahead and tell the detective how you were the victim in all of this. That's what you want everybody to believe, right?" He elbowed me in the ribs, and I doubled over in pain.

I coughed twice, blinked back tears, and fought waves of nausea. Clive stepped back and looked surprised. I felt Loncar's hand on my back.

"You okay?"

I held up my hand, and then slowly, I stood. "I'll survive."

"You're done here," Loncar said to Clive.

"I'll expect copies of your photos in my inbox this afternoon," Gigger added.

Clive looked back and forth between their faces. "That's not the arrangement. You can't revoke my access."

"Mr. Barrington, I've been over your contract. Page four, third paragraph. Ms. Ries retained the right to replace you," Loncar said. For the briefest of moments, I saw him as my hero and overlooked his unfortunate cuff choice.

"That's right. If she wants to replace me, she's the one who has to do it. Not you," Clive said. "And not him." He pointed to Gigger.

A light bulb went off in my head. "Amanda already retained a new photographer." All three men looked at me. "Dante Lestes. I know you saw him at the show. He was sitting next to me when you took the photos before the show started. You waved at him, and then you went backstage. Come to think of it, that was right before the fire started."

"If Amanda wants to replace me, she should have told me."

Clive's elbow-to-the-injury move had left me angry and vindictive, and I hit him where it hurt. "She did. Maybe you were mad at her and set the fire yourself? As a way to get back at her?"

Clive looked like he'd bitten into a rotten lemon. He turned and spit onto the gravel behind him. "I don't have to listen to your accusations." He put his camera in a black nylon duffle bag.

Loncar looked at me. "Do I know this Mr. Lestes?"

"I don't think so. But I can arrange an introduction if you'd like."

Loncar studied me for a few seconds and then turned to Clive. "Mr. Barrington, I'm going to follow up with Ms. Ries, and I suggest you do the same."

The cockiness that had come with Clive's all-access pass vanished, and in its place was a scowl. I thought back to what Dante had told me about Clive. Was he a predator among the models? Most of them could take care of themselves, but Harper had been the loner. Had he been after her? Would my constant interference have angered him enough to assault me in the parking lot?

I knew he'd be calling Amanda sooner rather than later, and if she was in a vulnerable state, he would convince her she needed him. I had to get to her first and explain why it would be a very bad idea for Clive Barrington to remain part of her inner circle. The good news was Dante could step in without missing a beat, as long as he had nothing else on his plate.

"Detective, you don't need me to stick around, do you?" I asked Loncar. He looked at me like he thought I was nuts. "I just remembered I have to make a couple of phone calls, and you probably have things to do here. I imagine you don't want anybody who isn't on the force hanging around trying to figure things out on their own."

"Not so fast," he said. He looked past me at Clive and didn't speak until after the photographer had backed out of his space, turned around to glare at us, and driven away. "I'm going to get Ms. Kidd's statement," he said to Gigger. The arson investigator nodded and walked away.

"New partner?" I asked.

"Ms. Kidd, my superiors think last night's fire was an accident. I don't want to encourage you, but I don't agree with them."

"How would that encourage me?"

"I have no authority here. Inspector Gigger is an arson investigator for the Pennsylvania Arsonists Association. He's using my office and my resources. He has full cooperation from the department. As far as my captain is concerned, there is no ongoing criminal investigation from our office."

"There was a fire here last night, and Amanda told me about the threats to her company."

"What threats?"

"Letters that somebody's been sending her. She said she told the police about them."

"First I've heard of them."

"Amanda showed them to me. I don't know if it's related, but two nights ago I was attacked backstage at her rehearsal. Then there was the fire. I think the two things are connected. Even if she hadn't confided in me, I'd be looking for answers."

"She confided in you? Why would she do that?"

"I don't think she trusts anybody else. No offense."

A few beats of silence passed between us. I hadn't planned on making it sound like Loncar couldn't do his job. Truth was, I knew he could, but now hardly seemed the time to offer an apology. Perhaps a nice manly arrangement of flowers delivered to the precinct tomorrow would be better.

"I can advise you to mind your own business, but since there's no investigation, I can't do much about it if you don't."

"You always tell me to mind my own business. You tell me to steer clear of your investigation for my own good. This time, I've already been attacked and hospitalized before there even was an investigation."

He wiped his arm across his brow. "Officially, I have nothing to say. Unofficially? You're in dangerous territory, and there's pretty much nothing I can do about it."

10

SHOULD HAVE SAID NO

"You just said you had no authority here, but I bet you want to know what happened, right?" I said. "I was here. I've been here all along. Whoever attacked me told me to stay out of it. That means somebody thinks I know something about something. And I bet that something has to do with whatever happened here. I bet I could help you. Ask me something. Go ahead, ask."

He glared at me. "As much as I hate to admit it, you've got a knack for this stuff. And after that article on you in the paper, my boss won't get near you with a ten-foot pole. He says you're making us look bad. Just do me a favor? If you figure anything out, keep me in the loop."

I'd experienced a certain amount of notoriety since moving back to Ribbon, and what at first seemed like a case of bad timing had turned into a mild celebrity status. Carl Collins, reporter for the *Ribbon Times*, had done a small profile on me after I'd saved the local museum considerable embarrassment over an exhibit of hats on loan from a Hollywood actress. I leveraged my newfound local fame into a side gig. When not working for Amanda, I acted as personal shopper and stylist to Ribbon's fashion challenged. It covered my immediate budgetary needs and allowed me to splurge on the occasional heavily discounted off-season garment at the Ribbon Outlet Center. Even Logan had traded up in his quality of life, his kitty bed now lined in cast-off cashmere sweaters beyond repair.

"No problem." I looked behind me at where Clive's car had been. My announcement that he'd been replaced had started a ticking clock, and I needed to talk to Amanda and Dante. "Detective, I have to go," I said. I waited another second to see if he had any last words of warning for me and hopped back and forth from foot to foot so he'd think I had to pee.

"Be careful, Ms. Kidd," he said.

I drove half a mile down the street, pulled the car over to the shoulder, and called Amanda. After four rings, her service picked up. I hesitated before talking. What if Nick was still there? What if Tiny heard the message? I hung up and redialed. This time she answered.

"Amanda Ries Studio," she said.

"This is Samantha. Can you talk?"

"What is this in reference to?" Her tone was curt.

I guessed from her answer that she was not alone. "I found Clive Barrington lurking around Warehouse Five. There were cops too. One I know. The other was an arson investigator. I sort of made it sound like you had replaced Clive with another photographer."

"Please hold," she said. I was treated to a soft jazz version of a Billy Idol song, which was almost as offensive as her rudeness. She picked back up before the song ended. "I'm back. I'm sorry about that back there, but Nick was here. I told him it was Tiny on the phone."

"Where is he now?"

"He just left. Tell me what's going on."

"Okay." I told Amanda about Clive's presence at Warehouse Five but left out the part about Detective Loncar having no authority at the crime scene. Loncar felt like an unlikely ally, but in a way, I felt a loyalty to him. Weird. "Clive said you granted him unlimited access. Is that true?"

"Yes. When we started the whole thing. Tiny set it up. She said, depending on what pictures he took, we could use them for publicity. She had to get him access to the warehouse for when we weren't there, too, because he said there would be times when he wanted the quiet before the storm, you know, when none of us were there. There's not much he hasn't seen."

"That means Clive could have gotten into the warehouse and rigged the platform before your show."

"Why would he do that?"

"I'm not asking why yet. I'm just asking if he could."

"Sure, he could. But so could a lot of people. Your friend Eddie had access too. Tradava loaned me the mannequins that sat in the lobby. And the food service people came in early, and there are other artists that show their work in Warehouse Five, so they could have gotten in—"

"I only want to know about Clive right now. Has he given you any footage so far? Any preliminary photos to approve?"

"He gave Tiny some preliminary backstage shots to use early on. She handled everything that didn't involve the actual collection so I wouldn't have to be bogged down in details. She has his contract."

"Can you get it to me?"

"Sure. Is that all?"

"No. Dante Lestes is going to be your new photographer." I chewed my lower lip and debated whether to tell Amanda the truth about Dante. "He's a legitimate photographer, and you can trust him." I arranged to come by her office tomorrow morning and ended the call. Phase one, complete.

I started the Stingray and headed back to my house. The smell of my clothes was making me ill. Or maybe it was something else. Maybe it was the truth about my life starting to sink in.

Since the breakup with Nick, I'd been keeping myself busy, trying not to think about how things had gone wrong. But trading one relationship for another didn't feel right either. I hadn't mourned Nick and my breakup, and a part of me wondered if a meltdown was lingering under the surface.

Six weeks ago, things had been great. Nick and I had moved into steady-date-Saturday-night territory, and I'd stupidly traded on our relationship and asked him to put me on his payroll.

Nick was a high-end shoe designer. He had started his career working for a few top designers and eventually landed a position as creative director for a French couture house which was expanding from apparel into the accessories market. After he'd built up a name for himself, he literally sold off that name to a couple of financiers. He'd received professional recognition and cemented his fan base but felt he'd lost some of his creative control.

Nick had been one of the designers in my vendor matrix when I worked for Bentley's New York. There'd been chemistry from the first time we met in front of his showroom, but our positions in the industry kept us on our respective sides of the don't-cross line. It wasn't until after I left Bentley's and moved to Ribbon that we reconnected. He had bought back distribution of his company and invested every dime he had into a relaunch of his brand. I'd given up my lucrative career at Bentley's to become the trend specialist at Tradava. By all measures, we were both experiencing new beginnings, and the timing for a relationship finally seemed right.

And then we'd found the body of the man who had hired me, and I spent some time wondering if Nick was capable of murder. Turns out that's a biggie when it comes to determining if a relationship is on the horizon.

After that was cleared up—and after the six months he spent in Italy—I was ready to address my affections. Things were fine until I started working for him. Too much togetherness. Ultimately, we broke up.

And then he told me he'd given my name to Amanda to help with her runway show.

And now, forty-four days later, I was dealing with the aftermath.

Amanda Ries was everything I wasn't: classically beautiful, financially successful, and an upstanding law-abiding citizen who didn't question authority. She and Nick had gone to design school together. I still didn't quite believe him when he said they never had a romantic relationship. She was Barbie-doll pretty, with sleek black hair that fell to her waist and proportions that didn't come from pizza and meatball sandwiches. I couldn't compete with someone like that. And because I wanted to prove that I was a class act, despite every instinct I had, I took the job.

The ironic thing was that I had to turn away business to

fulfill my commitment. But that's not what this was all about. Nick had asked me to help Amanda, and that had felt good. He'd probably expected me to say no.

I should have said no.

I should have said no, pretended he'd never asked, and gone about my business.

But I didn't. Because Amanda, aside from being Nick's maybe-former girlfriend, was a talented designer, and after a year of false starts in jobs that fell short of my own expectations, I recognized that working with her would allow me to fall back on my passion for the industry. I had a high-taste level, proven instincts on trends, and was a good at multitasking. Besides, confronting my pettiness about Amanda's relationship with Nick was like putting a pin in it. At least that's what I'd hoped.

I pulled up in front of my house. I'd been planning to park the Stingray in the garage, but a brown minivan was in the driveway. I drove past the house, pulled into my neighbor's driveway, backed out, and parked by my mailbox.

A disheveled woman in a hooded coat stood by the door to my garage. "Samantha Kidd?" she asked.

"Yes."

She pushed the hood off her head. "I'm Molly Diers. I need help. I would have made an appointment, but I finally got a sitter, and it's an emergency. Can we do this?"

It took the better part of a minute for my brain to switch gears from arson and attack to the styling needs of my small town. If the woman in front of me hadn't appeared so in need of fashion help, I might not have ever made the connection.

Molly Diers wore an oversized olive-green snorkel coat over a pair of pants printed with superheroes. Her feet were shod in dirty camel Ugg boots that had seen better days, and there was a smudge of something green on her cheek.

"Follow me," I said. I unlocked the garage door and walked across the concrete floor to the door that opened at the top of the basement. A wooden staircase led down to my converted home office.

When I first moved back into the house, the basement had held several mismatched bookcases filled with magazines, memorabilia, and paint cans. The basement had flooded, thanks to my parents never having the foundation sealed, and most of the contents had been damaged to the point of ruin. I'd arranged for a trash pick-up and tossed everything but the clothes I made in high school.

Once emptied, I was left with a twenty-foot-long room with exposed brick walls. Five packs of yellow rubber gloves, several bottles of vinegar, a jug of bleach, and an industrial fan had removed traces of the flooding. Now the walls were decorated with fashion sketches, the room where my dad had brewed his homemade wine had been turned into a fitting room, and the rest of the space had been outfitted with bars for clothing samples and shelves for accessories. A discarded architect's table served as my desk.

Molly followed me down the stairs. I flipped to a blank page on a yellow legal pad.

"Have a seat. Let's talk about what you want."

"That's easy. I want to look good again. You should have seen me back in the day. Fashion was my life. I've been married for seven years, and the bastard left me. After two boys, I don't even feel like a woman anymore."

I jotted *single mother-seven years-woman* on the legal pad and underlined "woman" three times. "Tell me about your daily routine."

"I get up, feed the hellions, get them off to school. Five hours later I pick them up."

"What do you do all day?"

"I pick Cheerios out of my hair." I considered writing that part down. "Do you have kids?" she asked.

"No."

"Then you don't understand. You have no idea what a terror two boys can be. They wreck everything. Everything. Meanwhile, my rat ex-husband already has a new girlfriend half his age. He gets the boys every other weekend and the boys think he's a god. What do I do all day? Once I get them off to school, the house is quiet. I can relax. I have five hours to pretend my life turned out differently."

Molly Diers didn't need a stylist, she needed a therapist. "How do you dress now?" I asked.

"You're looking at it. If it doesn't have an elastic waist, I'm not interested."

I felt like I was on the *Punk'd* version of *What Not to Wear.*

"I have to be honest, Molly. I don't think we're going to be much of a match, style-wise."

"You can't turn me away. I need tough love. I read about you in the paper. You take on killers and whackos and police, and you lived in New York. When I was fourteen, I used to walk around my house with a book on my head. These days, high fashion is a T-shirt without a stain. Besides, the boys are back in school, and I need to look like I can hold down a job. I need you."

Already I felt bad for turning her down. I looked at my calendar. Amanda's name had been written in, but that job ended with the runway show. I flipped the page to next week and the week after that. All clear. If it wasn't for Molly Diers, what would I be doing? Looking for arsonists, flirting with Dante, and pining away over Nick.

Maybe I needed Molly Diers too.

"Fill out this questionnaire, and then let's set up a schedule for you."

I handed her a clipboard with a couple sheets of paper on it. Molly looked relieved. I pulled three tissues out of a box on the corner of my desk and handed them to her. "There's something green on your cheek."

"There's always something green on my cheek." She scrubbed her cheekbone until the green went away, leaving fresh pink skin.

I didn't know how other personal stylists worked, but when I hung out my shingle, I assumed I could figure it out as I went. I compiled binders of looks that represented the fashion identities I'd once learned from a Cosmo quiz: Casual, Fashion Forward, Bohemian, and Powerful. My personal style ran along the lines of whimsy, but my goal wasn't to have my clients dress like me.

I sat Molly in a comfy purple velvet chair and handed her a stack of binders. Day One involved identifying the way she wanted to dress, the sizes she wore, and the budget she had in mind. I'd shop and put together what I felt was the basis for a new wardrobe to suit her needs. My take was ten percent of her spend.

While she was busy with the binders, I snuck off to the back corner of the basement and called Dante.

"Where are you?" he asked.

"I'm at my house."

"I thought we had an arrangement."

"No, you had an arrangement. I had a need to change my clothes and see my cat. I'll be done here soon." I glanced at

Molly. She had her nose buried in Bohemian. "Can you come over in about an hour?"

"Sure."

Molly and I finished our first consultation, and she wrote me a check to cover my initial consulting fee. I thanked her, we set up an appointment three days away, and I walked her out. Dante's motorcycle pulled into the driveway next to her car as we were saying goodbye.

"Is he yours?" she asked.

"I'm not sure."

"I don't think I'll ever be ready for a man like that."

That made two of us.

11

ULTERIOR MOTIVES

I waited until Molly drove away before I led Dante into the house.

"You rang?" he asked.

I held my finger up in a just-a-minute gesture. I was hungry. I opened and closed cabinets looking for food and came up with a box of Snyder's of Hanover sourdough pretzels. I pulled a fat pretzel out and held the box toward Dante. He waved them off. I bit into the round loop of a full pretzel and leaned back against the counter.

"I talked to Amanda today," I said. "She's been getting threats at her studio."

"What threats?"

"Written. They look like old-fashioned ransom notes with letters cut out of magazines, but whoever made them kept the original and sent her a copy. I'm guessing it's because whoever did it didn't want to leave fingerprints."

"Nobody's going to take the time to cut letters out of a magazine."

"They did. I saw them. The most recent said 'Burn, baby,

burn!' I don't think it's much of a coincidence that her runway show went up in a blaze of glory."

Dante leaned back against the chair. "Why are you still helping Amanda?"

"Because I said I would. I made a commitment."

"The job is over."

Breakup Rule #4: Don't get into your last relationship problems with the potential new guy. Logan was the only one who heard the gory post-breakup details. Maybe if Dante and Logan bonded enough, I could leave the explanation to my cat.

"The fire investigator is trying to determine whether the runway fire was an accident or arson. Even if it was intentional, nobody was hurt, so it's not a homicide investigation."

"Have you talked to any of the models?"

"No."

"Not even Harper? Weren't you two close?"

"Harper was a loner among the girls. We weren't close, but she didn't seem to have any other friends. Besides, Harper is in Mexico. Why?"

"Samantha, I can understand your desire to figure this out, but there's something else driving you here, and you're not telling me what it is."

I looked down at my hands. "The attack was personal. Someone was in the parking lot waiting for me. Someone wanted to hurt me, and I don't know why."

"You might never know why."

"How am I supposed to move on if I don't know if it'll happen again? How do I know somebody isn't watching me every time I leave my house?"

"All the more reason to stay at my place."

"I'm not going to hide," I said. "But I can't live my life constantly looking over my shoulder either. I don't know how anybody could expect me to."

"What's your plan?"

"My plan?"

"I figure after your meeting with Amanda you came up with a plan. You asked me here because I'm a part of it." He stared at me for a few seconds. Logan climbed from the table onto Dante's leg and then onto the ground. Dante never broke eye contact with me. "Unless I'm wrong, and I wouldn't mind being wrong."

I felt my face grow warm. "I told Amanda to fire Clive and bring you on as her photographer. I need somebody on the inside. Clive was at Warehouse Five today—"

"You went to Warehouse Five? That's a crime scene."

"I know. Detective Loncar was there with an arson investigator."

"I can't imagine either one of them was happy with you walking around."

"Happy? No, but after Clive elbowed me in the ribs, Loncar took my side."

"He what?" Dante gripped the table and his knuckles turned white. His sleeves rode up, and the flame tattoos around his wrists throbbed with his pulse.

I waved my hand. "It's good that he did. I don't think the detective believed me until he saw I was in pain."

Dante looked like he wanted to put his fist through something. Maybe a wall, maybe Clive's face.

"He's out of the picture. You're in his place. Can you do that?"

"You said Clive was hired to document the show from inception to completion? Sure, I can step in."

"You'll need to get pictures of whatever you can if we're going to crack this thing."

He leaned back. "I'll get pictures of samples, sketches, and Amanda's showroom. If she'll give me a list of everybody she employed, I'll get interviews on film. Clive probably turned something over to her already. That's standard procedure."

I didn't know what to say. I'd gotten so used to everybody telling me I shouldn't be involved that I wasn't prepared for Dante to take me seriously. "Is that okay?" Dante asked.

"Sure."

"Great. I'll tell her I need to see whatever he's done so I can stay true to the style of the initial photography and keep the change of photographers seamless." He sat back in the chair and put his hands behind his head. "That should give us a good start if we're going to 'crack this thing.'" He smiled.

"Take pictures of everything you can. The fire happened after the attack. Did I see something backstage, and the fire was set to cover it up, or was someone planning to set the fire, and they wanted me gone before it happened?"

"You need to be careful. If you're right and somebody targeted you, they're not going to like knowing you're poking around their business."

"I know."

We stared at each other for a few seconds, until I broke eye contact and focused on my pretzel. I snapped off the other loop and bit into it. Pretzel dust covered the front of my shirt. I dusted it off, chewed, and swallowed the lump of dough. I felt better already.

"What now?" Dante asked.

"You need to go to Amanda's studio, introduce yourself, and get the lay of the land. She doesn't know I confided in you. Right now, she thinks you're a fashion photographer who can replace Clive."

"I'm your man on the inside."

"That's what I'm counting on. Be on the lookout for Tiny, Amanda's business manager, and anybody else who comes along. There was a tall black man there today named Oscar LeVay. He owns the agency where Tiny hired the models, and he expects Amanda to pay him seventy-five grand for the show even though it didn't take place. He may have taken the letters from Amanda's desk."

Dante's eyebrows went up.

"I was hiding behind a screen when Oscar arrived. When he left, the letters were gone."

"If she went to the police about the letters, they would have kept them."

"Maybe that's why the ones I saw were copies."

"Did you see this Oscar guy take them?"

"No. I don't even know if he saw them. But if he saw them, and he was responsible for sending them in the first place, he might take them to hide the evidence."

"Did you tell Amanda that?"

"No."

"Why not?"

Because Nick was there. "The timing wasn't right," I said out loud.

"Anything else you can tell me?"

"Clive wasn't happy when I dropped your name."

"You leave Clive to me."

I walked Dante to the front door. "Thank you for helping me," I said.

"Samantha, just because I'm helping you doesn't mean I don't have ulterior motives."

"Meaning?"

He put his fingers on my chin, tipped my head back, and kissed me. On the few occasions when I thought about what it would be like to kiss Dante, I imagined heat-of-the-moment, back-up-against-a-wall type stuff. Like kissing Brando in *The Wild One.*

It was just like I'd imagined.

The world melted into nothingness, and the room spun, leaving me dizzy. It was enough to make me forget the name of that shoe designer who'd been on my mind a lot lately. When Dante pulled away, he looked me straight in the eyes. I blinked twice and then looked down at his chest. He pulled on his motorcycle helmet, flipped the visor down, and left.

I took a shower, put on clean undies, and checked my reflection in the foggy mirror. My injuries, though invisible, felt like a corset around my waist, and the elastic on my panties dug into my chicken finger, ice cream, and waffle weight gain. I moved my gaze from my torso to my face. The person staring back at me looked like a stranger. Where was the happy- go-lucky buyer who turned projects in on time and hit her end-of-quarter target inventory levels? Where was the overachiever who met sell-through expectations and gross margin goals? Where was the woman who could travel three cities on the contents of one carry-on suitcase and stay under the company per diem of sixty dollars a day?

She was gone, a distant memory. In her place was an unemployed job seeker with a muffin top.

Since moving to Ribbon, I'd been suspected of murder, used as a plant in a counterfeiting ring, and trapped in a museum. I'd started a relationship I had long daydreamed about and was pretty much responsible for sabotaging it before it got off the ground. My friends had gone ignored since the attack. Life as I knew it was out of control. I hadn't even called my parents in California to tell them I'd been hospitalized. I didn't want to give anybody any reason to criticize my life. I was becoming isolated. And somewhere along the way, that had become okay.

As the fog cleared from the mirror, I focused on my reflection. I looked older than I had when I worked at Bentley's, and it had only been a little over a year. My brown hair hung past my shoulders, limp, unkempt. I'd gone from maintenance trims every six weeks to pulling it into a ponytail and ignoring it. My eyes looked tired. My brows needed shaping. My skin looked dull. And don't get me started on my pedicure.

I ran a thick comb through my hair and secured it into two low ponytails on either side of my head. Without stopping to overthink things, I picked up a pair of scissors and sliced through the hair on the left side of my head. *Whack!* Right below chin level. The hair bobbed up around my face. The right side of my hair was long, serious, and staid in comparison.

I held my hand up to cover the left hand side of the mirror. The person who stared back at me with long straight hair was a stranger. She had seen things I never expected to see and had lived through things I never expected to live through. She looked light-years older than I'd been when I moved back into this house.

I moved my hand to cover the right-hand side of the mirror. The woman I saw looked fresh. Perky. Ready for anything. Unfettered by straightening irons and blow driers and the fight against killers and naturally curly hair.

I took the scissors to the ponytail on the right and

snipped through the wet hair. The natural curls sprung up, making the hair instantly wavy. I squirted a handful of mousse into my palm and rubbed it onto my strands. I followed with a tinted moisturizer, mascara, and dark red lipstick, and blow-dried my hair upside down. When I flipped back up, I looked at the stranger in front of me. She looked like someone who didn't care so much that she'd been in the hospital two nights ago. She looked like she might have a plan. I didn't have a plan, so I liked the girl in the mirror even more.

I dressed in pajamas and went to the kitchen for a glass of wine. So what if it was only three thirty? That was practically happy hour. I downed the first glass and poured a refill. After the second, I had a good idea. I would call Nick. Just to say hi.

I ignored the voice that said two glasses of wine plus one call to an ex-boyfriend was not only a not good idea, it was plain old bad math. When his message came on, I pulled myself together. "Hi, Nick. It's Samantha." I stopped. What was I thinking? I ended the call and stared at the phone.

That went well. Not.

Seconds later my cell buzzed with a text: *Sorry didn't answer. At Brothers Pizza. Come join if you're not busy.*

I tried to text back something that communicated that I missed him and was looking forward to seeing him but not let on that I'd kissed Dante. I ended up going with: *See you soon.*

I stood up and stumbled. Maybe it hadn't been a good idea to drink wine on a stomach filled only with pretzels. And maybe it wouldn't be a good idea to drive to Brothers Pizza. How far away was it? I rolled my eyes up while I tried to calculate if I could walk, lost balance, and landed on the sofa. No, maybe it wasn't a good idea to walk either.

I called Eddie. "Yo," I said when he answered. "Do you want to go to Brothers?"

"Can't. I'm pulling an all-nighter at Tradava. Pizza does sound good, though."

"I'm meeting Nick, and I could use some backup."

"Did he call you, or did you call him?"

"I called him."

"And?"

"And he texted back and told me to join him." I waved my hand around, not necessary since he couldn't see me. "I just want to talk to him."

"About what?"

"Nothing."

"Are you okay?"

I spun around and caught my reflection in the microwave. The stranger who might have a plan looked back at me. "I'm great. I chopped off all my hair," I said. And then I hiccupped.

"Dude, don't go anywhere. I'll be there in ten minutes."

12

CAKE WITHOUT ICING

 moved around to the left, right, and top of my head.

"You weren't kidding," he said. "Follow me." He charged inside and started up the stairs.

"Aren't we getting pizza?"

"Not yet."

"Where are we going?"

"The bathroom." I stopped halfway up the stairs. He reached the landing and turned around. "How to put this gently," he said, drumming his fingers on his chin. "The right side of your hair is an inch shorter than the left. Come on."

I climbed the remaining stairs and entered the bathroom behind him. My two chopped-off ponytails lay next to the sink like a sacrifice to the beauty gods. Eddie stared at them for a few seconds, shut the lid of the toilet, and instructed me to sit facing the wall. He combed my hair and separated it into sections. I felt him tug on the length, and then I heard a series of snip, snip, snips. He repeated the process toward the back left of my head and then the back right.

"Aren't you going to ask me why I did it?" I asked.

"Dude, someone put you in the hospital a couple of days ago, you almost got burned down at Amanda's runway show, and you're fresh from a breakup with Nick. So you freaked out. I'm surprised you didn't dye it purple."

He tipped my head forward, and I felt the cold metal scissor blades against the back of my neck.

"Do you know what you're doing?" I asked.

"I style the mannequin wigs at Tradava. Now, sit still and shut up."

Eddie lined up the jagged edges of my butchered haircut. I hiccupped again.

"What have you eaten today?"

"Wine and pretzels. Are you almost done back there?" I waved my hand around behind my head, feeling the layers.

He swatted my hand away and set the comb and scissors on the counter. Like an expert stylist, he threaded his fingers into the back of my hair and shook it from side to side. "Turned out pretty well, all things considered."

"Great. Let's go." I stood up and swung my leg over the toilet seat like I was dismounting a horse.

"You might want to put on clothes first," he said, pointing to my pajamas.

I went to my bedroom while Eddie went downstairs. In my closet, I shoved my collection of candy-colored pumps to the side and stared at a pair of Doc Martens I'd bought in the nineties. Black leather lined in red plaid. They were tough. They were don't-mess-with-me shoes. That's what I needed. I also needed a don't-mess-with-me outfit.

I changed into an oversized red V-neck sweater that I turned backward, and a pair of black skinny jeans. I looked in the mirror at my reflection. My hair was already mostly dry, hanging in waves around my head.

Something was off. I found a black beaded necklace shaped to look like a peter pan collar and tied it around my neck. Long black ribbons dangled down my exposed back. I folded the cuffs of the Docs down so the red plaid lining showed.

"What's taking you so long?" Eddie called up the stairs.

I knew exactly what was taking me so long. The wine buzz was wearing off, and in its place was self-consciousness. What had I intended to accomplish by calling Nick? If I was being honest with myself, I'd say I wanted attention. I wasn't ready to be honest just yet.

I jogged down the stairs, gave Logan a can of Fancy Feast, ate another pretzel to calm my nerves, and we left.

It took seven minutes to get to Brothers Pizza. On a good day, when the lights cooperated with my need for cheese and dough, I could get there in four. Tonight, I welcomed the additional three. They gave me a chance to cycle through all the potentially disastrous outcomes for the evening.

"Why did I think this was a good idea?" I said to Eddie.

"Because you like drama, and you thrive on chaos."

"It was a rhetorical question."

We crossed the lot and went inside. Eddie wasn't used to me walking so fast (thank you, Docs) and had to jog to keep up with me. I pulled the door open and waited a second for my eyes to adjust to the dim interior.

Brothers was my favorite pizza place in all of Ribbon. They had opened in 1971 and appealed to every generation of locals since then. The interior was classic old-school Italian, with Chianti flasks and plastic ivy hanging from the ceiling. The wallpaper was pink flocked with burgundy. The configuration was long and narrow, with booths on the right-hand side, tables on the left, and a couple of pinball machines next to sliding-glass doors that led to the outside seating. An internet juke box, the only modern addition to the place, stood next to the bar, halfway to the back.

Booths were red vinyl and tables were wood. Initials, expressions, and a couple of phone numbers were carved into most of them. The seven pizza ovens were in constant use and contributed to the scent of tangy tomato sauce, oregano, and basil. They probably had the fixings for a salad around somewhere, but I'd never seen anyone order one.

"Shoe designer, ten o'clock," Eddie said. "Oh no, he didn't. Let's go." Eddie grabbed my arm and tried to spin me around. The treads on my boots made me unspinnable.

"What?" I asked. I scanned the interior and spotted Nick and Amanda together by the Ms. Pac-Man machine. I had the top score on that back in high school. Focus, Samantha. "He brought Amanda? He didn't say anything about her being here with him."

"What exactly did he say?"

I pulled out my phone and scrolled through the texts. "At Brothers. Come join."

"That's what I thought. You know, because texting is so good for nailing down specifics of a post-breakup rendezvous." He took my phone, deleted the text, and handed it back. "You wanted this, right?" He gave me a push.

I turned away and grabbed his bicep. "I don't want it to look like I called you for moral support. I'm going to play it cool. Pretend we met up in the parking lot and you're getting takeout."

"Fine." Eddie split off from me and stood in line at the ordering counter. I watched Nick and Amanda. They appeared not to have noticed me yet. He said something to her, and she laughed. He put his hand on her shoulder. She didn't shrug it off.

No way was I going over there now. Not gonna happen.

I turned and headed back to the exit. Eddie stood in a crowd by the ordering counter. I flashed him a look and jerked my thumb toward the door. He shook his head no and pointed to the pizza oven and then at his watch. I turned around and went outside.

A blast of cool air hit my face. I couldn't leave; Eddie had driven me. And I wasn't about to walk the two miles home, even if I was wearing comfortable shoes. I looked at the moon and then looked at my phone. There was one other option.

I texted Dante and suggested if he wasn't busy, he join me for pizza. He texted back almost immediately. Now, all I had to do was wait outside until he showed up. And then, I'd be on a date too.

The door to Brothers opened, and Nick came outside. "Kidd," he said.

"Taylor," I said back, opting to act like we were in fifth grade.

"I almost didn't recognize you. You look different." He smiled, and the crinkles at the corners of his root-beer-barrel-colored eyes deepened. "New haircut," he added.

"I needed a change."

"Change can be good."

He reached up as if he were going to push my hair away from my face like he'd done so many times before. I put my hand palm-side out and stopped him before he touched me. The smile dropped from his face. We stared at each other as if there was something to be said, but neither one of us knew where to start.

"How's the job hunt going?" he asked.

"Great. But I'm guessing I shouldn't count on you for a reference."

"Come on. You know it wasn't like that."

"No, I guess it wasn't. But hey, thanks for recommending me to Amanda." I held both thumbs up and gave him a fake smile. "That's sure to head somewhere great."

He grabbed my wrist and pulled me around the side of the building. I looked over my shoulder at the parking lot. No signs of Dante.

"If you have something you want to say, then go ahead and say it," he said.

"Me? What could I have to say? The last actual conversation we had was you telling me to turn my back on Eddie in his time of need. But now it's your friend with the crisis. What do you want me to do now, Nick? Ignore Amanda's problems and watch somebody destroy her business?"

Nick's eyes flashed. "It's not the same thing."

"You're right. It's not. Because this time you *asked* me to help her."

"And I've felt guilty about that ever since."

"Well, don't. None of this is for you or for her. I'm only trying to figure out who attacked me. Maybe nobody else cares about that, but I do. Saving Amanda's business would be icing on the cake, but you know something?" I put both hands on his chest and pushed him back. "I can totally eat cake without icing."

He looked at me as if I'd turned blue and told him I planned to live under a mushroom. "Kidd, you're not making any sense."

Did I just say something about eating cake without icing?

I sensed that righteous indignation was a limited resource that would soon give way to tears. I would not let Nick see me cry. I would not let him know how I'd felt when the days after our last conversation turned into weeks. When I'd been in the hospital and he hadn't even sent me a card.

"Samantha?" Dante said behind me. I looked over my shoulder and smiled. He approached us and put his hands on either side of my waist. "You didn't have to wait outside for me." He looked at Nick and then back at me. "How about I go get us a booth?"

"Sure. I'll be done in a second."

The bells over the door chimed as Dante disappeared inside. I turned back to Nick. The crinkles were gone from his eyes. "Kidd," he said. "I never expected things to get so complicated." He bent down and kissed my cheek. "Take care of yourself."

He went back in, leaving me out front. Seconds later, Eddie came outside with a white pizza box.

"Dude? Are you okay?"

A single tear dropped from my eye and left a cold track over my cheek. I swiped it away. "I know you have to get back to Tradava, but I'm not ready to leave yet."

"I saw Dante come in. Are you responsible for that too?"

I nodded. "Go. I'll be fine. I'll catch a ride home with him."

"I hope you know what you're doing."

I pushed through the doors, scanned the interior, and found Dante seated at a booth in the back. I snaked through the crowd and lowered myself onto the opposite side. The wine buzz from earlier was wearing off, but under the circumstances, I knew it would be a good idea to order something to eat.

"Hey," I said.

"Hey yourself," he answered. "New look?"

I reached up and felt the new shorter ends of my hair. "I needed a change."

"With just your hair or with other things too?"

"I'm considering a total lifestyle overhaul."

A beer sat on a cardboard Bud Light coaster on the table. The glass was more full than empty. I glanced at it and then at him.

"Why'd you want me to meet you here, Samantha?"

I shrugged. "I needed an excuse to get out of the house."

"I don't think that's the reason."

"Okay, fine. I like their pizza."

"You picked a fine time to start telling the truth." This time he smiled.

A waiter carried a silver tray to our table. "Large round with cheese, right?" he said to me.

"This can't be ours. We haven't ordered yet."

The waiter set the pizza on the table. "Missy, you've been ordering the same thing since you were in high school." He looked at Dante. "Good luck with this one. She's been breaking hearts for two decades." He left.

Dante transferred a slice onto a beige plastic plate for me and then for himself. I shook on a generous amount of oregano and bit into the tip of the slice. Too hot. Burnt my mouth. I reached for the water and guzzled half of the glass. Dante watched me. I set my slice down and looked at him.

"It's hot," I said.

"I hear some like it hot."

"I heard that too."

"What about you, Samantha? How do you like it?"

"I like it room temperature."

He raised one eyebrow.

"Are we still talking about pizza?" I asked.

He smiled. "For now."

"I can live with that." I turned my attention back to the slice. I was reaching for my third when I realized Dante's second still sat on his plate.

"Go for it," he said.

"I can't eat a third slice if you're not going to at least pretend to finish your second."

"I have a better idea. Let's get a to-go box and get out of here."

"But—"

"Your friend Eddie asked if I could give you a ride home. And I said I would, but there's someplace we have to go first."

After packing the pizza up, I followed Dante out of Brothers. Out of the corner of my eye, I looked for Nick or Amanda but saw neither one. It was just as well. I wasn't sure what Dante had in mind, but I thought it best not to have the image of Nick in my mind when it happened.

Dante led me to a black sedan. He beeped a remote at it, and the lights flickered once.

"Isn't this your sister's car?" I asked.

"Yes. I don't want to draw attention to ourselves."

"What exactly do you have in mind?"

"We're working a case, Samantha." He rested his forearms on the top of the car and looked across the hood at me. "We're going back to the scene of the crime."

13

THE MAIN EVENT

ALL OVER THE WORLD, COUPLES WERE HEADING OUT TO DANCE clubs, bars, and restaurants for date night. Dante and I were headed to a crime scene.

Samantha Kidd, this is your life.

While I wondered what Dante's sister would say about the scent of pizza that would most certainly cling to the interior of her otherwise pristine car, Dante drove us to Warehouse Five. It was dark, and the roads were crowded. He parked the car under a streetlamp about a hundred feet away from the gravel lot I'd stood in earlier. The aches and pains I'd been ignoring all day were catching up to me, and I moved slowly. Dante was halfway to the building when he realized I was still by the car. He doubled back.

"You okay?"

"I'll manage. I think I'm getting stiffer as the night goes on."

"You need to exercise. Stretch. Stay limber."

"I exercise plenty," I lied. "I'll be fine. Let's go."

He reached for my hand and guided me forward. My

initial instinct was to shake him off, but I found it comforting to hold onto him. Even though he was ahead of me, he walked at a pace that I could match. He didn't let go when we reached the lot, and suddenly it seemed awkward to stand in a faintly lit parking lot with Dante holding my hand, like maybe this rendezvous was about more than searching for overlooked clues.

"You said Clive was here today?" Dante asked. I nodded. "Was he paying special attention to anything?"

"Hard to say. The building was locked, but he was inside. When he came out, he took pictures of the back door and windows. We're not going to be able to see anything he was looking at."

He turned toward the building, and I followed. Together we stumbled over the loose gravel, getting farther and farther from the car. Dante pulled a leather glove out of the inside pocket of his motorcycle jacket, let go of my hand, and pulled it on. He reached for the doorknob and jiggled it. Locked. He pulled on another glove and leaned close to the window, framing the light away from his eyes so he could see inside.

I stood on my tiptoes behind him and peeked over his shoulder. The only thing visible was a faint stationary light coming from somewhere to the left.

Dante looked at me. "See anything?"

"How am I supposed to see anything? It's dark out, and you're in my way. That's why I came here when there was daylight."

He unzipped his jacket and lifted a camera that hung around his neck.

"There was a guy in high school who wore a camera around his neck," I said. "I think it was a Warhol thing. Were you like that? The guy at the parties who caught all the embarrassing stuff on film? Or were you the *Sex, Lies, and Videotape* guy who…" I felt my face flush. "Never mind."

"When I went to a party, I wasn't all that concerned with taking pictures."

"Then why bring a camera tonight?"

"I'm on the job, see?" he said out of the corner of his mouth. He fiddled with the dial around the lens and aimed the camera at me. The shutter clicked a few times but there was no flash.

"Hey!" I said. "Stop that."

He faced the building, and the shutter clicked a few more times.

"Don't you want to turn on the flash or something?"

"Don't need to. I'm using infrared film."

"And this is good for us why?"

"This film captures a picture of the infrared spectrum, not what you see with your eyes. I can't develop it until I'm in a darkroom, but there's a chance we'll catch something nobody else will see either. Every day that goes by is a chance for the scene to get disrupted. Critters, wind, weather. If there's a clue here to whatever happened, we have to find it sooner rather than later. We're already working against a ticking clock."

"This film is going to help you figure out if Clive saw something before Detective Loncar asked him to leave."

"Yes."

"Have you been planning this all night?"

"I admit, your invitation took me by surprise, but after that, yes."

I didn't know if it was the solitude of the parking lot, the forethought of Dante's infrared camera plan, or the lingering romance of having shared a pizza, but I stepped closer to him. "Do you have anything else planned for tonight?" I asked quietly.

He stared at me for a second before he leaned down and kissed me. What I'd gotten earlier that day had been little more than a preview. Tonight, I was treated to the main event.

My arms went up, around the back of his neck, and pulled him closer. I parted my lips and felt his teeth gently bite at my lower lip. I tipped my head back and he kissed down the side of my neck and then back up to my ear lobe. If I hadn't been holding on to him, my legs would have given way underneath me.

He unbuttoned my coat and slipped his arms around me. I flinched when he touched a bruise. He pulled his arms away.

"Did I hurt you?" he asked in a low voice.

"The jerk who jumped me hurt me."

Dante held my hand and lowered himself to the gravel. He lifted the hem of my oversized red sweater with his gloved fingers and kissed the bruised flesh to the left and right of my navel. I closed my eyes. We were in the middle of a public parking lot, but it felt like the most secluded place in the world. I put my hands on his head and tipped it back so he was looking at my face.

"I'm not as tough as I act," I said.

He nodded a few times and looked again at my waist. He pulled the right glove off with his left hand and used his index finger to trace a line across my tummy. After about a minute, he pushed himself up to a standing position, put his bent knuckle under my chin, and tipped my head back again.

"That's why you've been breaking hearts since high school."

I expected him to kiss me again. He didn't. Instead, he took my hand and pulled me ever so gently toward the building. "I'm going to take as many pictures as I can. You said the police kicked Clive away from here and secured the scene?"

Dante's gears had shifted from romantic interlude to investigator on the job, and it took me a second to shake off the thought of his lips on mine and focus on his question. "Clive was inside the building when I got here. He must have seen me before I saw him. I walked up to the door, and he opened it and startled me. He didn't say where he'd been or what he was doing. I bet that camera gives him access to a lot of places, no questions asked."

Dante put his hand on his own camera. "That's what we're counting on." He looked up at the building. "What's on the other side?"

"The parking lot. I'm going to check on my car while we're here."

Truth was, I needed a couple of minutes away from Dante. His tender kisses had been unexpected, and now I was more mixed up than ever. I'd been attracted to him since our first meeting, but I'd been in a relationship with Nick. Now I wasn't. Or was I?

We'd broken up. And then I'd fallen apart. Now it seemed like there was a second shoe that still hadn't dropped. What did that scene at Brothers mean? Was he in or was he out?

I didn't know. I didn't like that I didn't know, but I didn't think it was a good idea to race from one man to another as long as I was confused about my feelings for both of them.

Nobody said I had to decide tonight. Healing takes time, and if I gave myself enough time, the answer was bound to present itself. At least that's what this month's advice column in *Elle* magazine said.

The corners of the parking lot were marked off with streetlamps, but the bulbs were out in two of them. The lot was dark. I knew I should be doing what Dante was doing: looking for clues related to the fire. But morbid curiosity led me to the exit I'd walked through before getting attacked.

I stood with my back pressed up against the solid metal door. Other entrances were more inviting; this one was intended for deliveries and crew members. The frame was flush with the door's surface. It would have disappeared into the exterior wall if not for the brass lock and partially rusted doorknob that now jutted into my left butt cheek.

I closed my eyes and thought back to the attack two days ago. What did I remember? I had been on my way outside. A few steps into the lot, and the flicker of a fire had caught my attention. Within seconds—or faster, maybe—the fire had connected with my foot like someone had drawn a line on the macadam. From that point, I hadn't had time to think. I'd swatted at the flames while a stranger approached and had been unprepared for the sudden beating with the bag of fruit.

I hadn't spent much time thinking about the choice of fruit as a weapon. Fruit would have been easy enough to come by. The food service table at Warehouse Five was filled with fresh fruit, raw vegetables, and Coke Zero. The soda went first then the vegetables. I'd heard a few of the girls whispering about the high sugar content in fruit and whether someone was trying to ruin their careers. I almost heard their minds blow the day I arrived with a hoagie.

But soft citrus as a weapon was intended to inflict injuries that could not be traced. Which told me whoever assaulted me hadn't been all that concerned with my wellbeing. If they'd hit a major organ, that warning might as well have been a death threat.

I walked to the edge of the lot where the paved parking spaces met with dirt and loose gravel. The lights were out, except for the glow of the red-orange Exit sign. If someone had determined a path for the fire from a pre-drawn trail of accelerant, would I be able to see it? Or would the traces of that trail have been eradicated by the firemen who had doused the building with water to put out the fire?

Dante was using infrared film to catch things we couldn't see, but there had to be other answers here. What else couldn't I see with my own eyes?

I dropped down to the ground and ran my gloved hand over the macadam. I lifted it to my nose and sniffed, expecting the scent of gasoline. All I got was a nose full of silvery cobwebs and gravel that stuck to my glove.

I stood up and slapped my hands together to rid them of the shiny, silk-like threads and pebbles. Again, I was struck with questions about my knowledge of Amanda's show and how that would make someone see me as a threat. I played out my last few hours as part of Amanda's team. Had Oscar been angered by how I lobbied on behalf of the models? Had Clive been using his position as photographer to conduct some other nefarious business? Had Santangelo arranged the attack because I was a part of Amanda's team? Had Amanda herself been planning a publicity stunt?

I opened my eyes and looked at my black Honda del Sol. The plastic top was in place, and the windshield was covered with colorful flyers and coupons for upcoming art shows, discount car washes, and at least a dozen other advertisements. It didn't seem like a good idea to leave the vehicle parked in the lot. I felt around in my handbag for my keys and unlocked the driver's side door. I cleared the flyers off the windshield and threw them onto the passenger-side seat.

It took a couple of tries to get the cold engine to turn over. When it caught, I put it into gear and locked the doors. Movement at the edge of the lot caught my eyes. I rolled down the dirty windows to get an unobstructed view outside.

Just like at the runway show, I smelled the fire before I saw it. I drove to the dumpster at the edge of the lot. Flames leapt up from inside the receptacle.

I saw a leg jutting out of the top a moment later.

14

PINKY SWEAR

I slammed on the brakes and jumped out of the car. Despite the cold of the night air, heat from the fire licked at my face and coated me in sticky, desperate fear.

"Samantha! Get away from the dumpster!" Dante called out. He ran toward me and waved his hand to the side.

"There's someone inside!" I yelled, pointing as close as I could to the leg.

"Get back!" He threw his arms around me from behind and turned me away from the fire. I screamed from the pain of his arms against my bruises. He half carried, half dragged me several feet away.

An explosion cracked like a boom of thunder. Pieces of trash sprayed through the air. Dante pulled me down to the gravel and shielded me with his shoulder. I pushed him away and scrambled to my feet. I pulled my cell phone from my bag and called 911.

The fire truck arrived before the police. Men in khaki jumpsuits with yellow reflective tape climbed from the vehicle, uncoiled a hose, and put out the flames. Dante sat next to me on the hood of my car. We were wrapped in a blanket I'd found in the trunk. Two black and whites pulled into the lot from the left, and the policemen conferred with the firemen. A dark brown sedan entered from the right, and Detective Loncar got out. He stared at the dumpster for a few seconds and then walked over to us.

"Let me do the talking," I said to Dante.

"Ms. Kidd, Mr. ..." Loncar paused.

"This is Dante Lestes. Dante, this is Detective Loncar. Dante is the photographer I was telling you about earlier today. The man who's going to take over for Clive Barrington."

Dante freed his arm from the blanket and shook Loncar's hand.

"Ms. Kidd, I know you know this is a crime scene. Care to tell me what you two are doing here?"

"I know you're not happy to see me, but before we get to that, you should know that there's a body in the dumpster. I was over there," I said, pointing behind me, "and I saw something move over there." I pointed to the trash receptacle. "I didn't see the flames until I got close. I also saw a leg. I called for Dante, and the dumpster went up like the Fourth of July."

Loncar patted his pockets until he found his small spiral-bound notebook. He scribbled something inside. "You say you saw movement before you saw the fire?"

"Yes. Honestly, I didn't even know that's what it was. That's why I went closer. When I saw the leg, I knew whoever was in there would get burned."

"How long would you say it was between you seeing something and the explosion?"

My eyes rolled up while I ran the memory through my

mind like an editor reviewing first rushes. "A minute, maybe. It happened quickly."

A shiny silver car pulled into the lot and parked catty-corner to Loncar's dirty sedan. Inspector Gigger got out. Loncar said something unrepeatable and told us to wait where we were. When he was a couple of steps away from us, I turned to Dante.

"The guy who looks like Ichabod Crane is in charge of the arson investigation at the fashion show. I don't think Loncar likes him. I don't like him either. At least with Loncar, I know where I stand."

"Where's that?"

"If he had his way, it would be a couple of miles from the crime scene."

"You don't seem to respect his wishes."

"I'm not the one who brought us here," I said.

"Point taken."

Loncar pointed to Dante and me, and Inspector Gigger looked at us, his expression unreadable. He popped his trunk, pulled out two bottles of water, and crossed the lot to where we sat on the hood of my car. Before he spoke, he handed each of us a bottle. I didn't realize how thirsty I was until I gulped down half the contents.

"Thank you," I said. I looked at Dante. He set his bottle next to him. It remained unopened.

After a lightning round of introductions, Gigger turned his attention to me. "Ms. Kidd, Detective Loncar tells me you were the one to call 911. Can you tell me what you saw?"

"I already told Detective Loncar everything I saw."

"But Detective Loncar isn't me, so why don't you go through it again?" he said. He flashed a tight smile that vanished as quickly as it had appeared. If I'd been on the fence about him earlier, there was no confusion now. Like Loncar, I didn't like the man, but there were bigger issues at present than a tally of Gigger's popularity votes.

"I came around the back of the building to check on my car. It's been here since the night I was attacked. Something by the dumpster caught my eye. I don't know what it was. I drove closer to check it out, and that's when I saw the flames. I yelled to Dante to meet me around the back—"

"Why?" he interjected.

"What?"

"Why did you call to your boyfriend?"

"He's not my boyfriend." I looked at Dante, who studied Gigger. "I saw movement by the dumpster. I thought maybe somebody needed help."

I felt Dante press his thigh into mine ever so slightly. It was a warning.

"Did you see anybody who might need help?" Gigger asked Dante.

"The bin exploded before I got close enough," he said.

"Yes or no. Did you see anybody?"

"No."

Gigger turned toward the dumpster and crossed his arms. "It's dark outside. You probably saw a rat."

I jumped down from the car and threw the blanket off my shoulders. "It wasn't a rat, Inspector. I don't like rats. If I saw one, I would have run the other way."

He stared at me for an uncomfortable number of seconds. I wanted to uncap my water and throw what was left of it in his face, but there wasn't enough to have any impact. Maybe that's why Dante was saving his.

Gigger turned to Dante. "You can't corroborate Ms. Kidd's statement. Is that correct?" Dante shook his head slowly. Gigger nodded at each of us and walked back to Loncar.

The firemen put out the fire. When they finished, they put the hose on the truck and stood around in the lot. I counted twelve men. Twelve pairs of thick men's boots stomping around the gravel close to the dumpster. Twelve pairs of size-twelve feet destroying any evidence that might have been left behind by the person who started the fire. I was thankful for the firemen's timely arrival and attention to detail in the form of putting out the flames, but I knew if there was something to be found, chances were, it had been destroyed.

Dante fussed with the zipper on his motorcycle jacket underneath the blanket. I climbed back up and wrapped the other side of the blanket around me. We sat side by side on the hood of the car, watching the scene in front of us. Gigger nodded to the head fireman and approached the dumpster. His hands were behind his back and his face was aimed at the ground. Slowly he walked around the base of the trash bin, swinging his head from left to right with each step he took.

"Tell me exactly what you saw," Dante said to me. "Start with what you were doing when you left my sight. Take your time."

I stared straight ahead and tried to find my chi. Since I didn't do yoga and wasn't sure what my chi was, I defaulted to a couple of calming breaths before speaking. Maybe yoga would be a good idea.

"I wanted to retrace my steps from the night I was attacked. I stood in the doorway with my back to the door and looked at my car and then slowly walked toward it. When I got there, I unlocked the door and put the flyers that were under the windshield wipers onto the passenger-side seat. I got in. Something by the dumpster caught my eye. I drove closer and rolled down the windows. I smelled something burning. Then the fire showed up from the top of the dumpster, and I saw the leg."

"I hate to have to ask this, but do you know if the leg was attached to a person?"

"You think it was just a leg? Sticking out of the dumpster?" Realization of what Dante suggested made me shudder like a team of cats had clawed a chalkboard nearby. "What if it's not there anymore? Do you think that's why someone set the fire? They amputated someone's leg, and they wanted to destroy the evidence? Should I tell Gigger?"

"Shhh," Dante said. "You told Loncar. Do you trust him?"

"I don't know if trust applies here. I think he'll follow up on what I said, but if Gigger is keeping him out of the investigation, then he's in pretty much the same boat as us. Unless—"

"Unless what?" Dante asked.

I reached inside the neckline of Dante's jacket and fingered the black nylon strap that held his camera around his head. "I would think the investigating officer would be very interested in the photos you took."

"That is a good point."

"But I think, since nobody asked us if we had any photos to share, that it might be best for us to see what's on your film before telling anybody."

"There are people who might say that's withholding evidence."

"Yes, but none of those people are here, right?" I searched Dante's face. "And I'll give the pictures to Loncar.

You don't even know if there's anything to show him. It's not like you were back here taking pictures. You were on the other side of the building. Wouldn't it be worse if you told him you had evidence, and it turned out there was nothing there?"

"I don't think 'worse' is the word you want."

"You know what I mean."

"Unfortunately, I do," he said.

"Then we're agreed? We'll see what's on the film, and then we'll turn it over to Loncar."

"You're not going to make me take a pinky swear, are you?"

"You think I'm the pinky-swear type?"

"The more I get to know you, the surer I am that you're a type all your own."

"I'm going to take that as a compliment," I said.

"Your choice."

Loncar pulled away from the group of firemen and rejoined us. "Ms. Kidd, I'm going to ask you a favor. Have Mr. Lestes drive you home."

"But my car's been here for two days now."

"I understand. I can't tell you not to drive it home, but until we have a chance to go over the scene in daylight, I'd prefer you left it here."

This was a different side of Detective Loncar. In the past, we'd gone round and round, me proclaiming what I knew, him testing me to see if I was making up a story. There had been times we collaborated, and there had been times when I'd gone rogue and caught a killer in his backyard.

This was the first time he had acted like I had some control over whether to grant his request. It might have been the effect of Gigger's condescending attitude, or it might have been the late hour. Or maybe Loncar was warming to me.

"Mr. Lestes, I think we have everything we need from you tonight." He pulled two cards with contact info from his wallet and held them out.

I waved the card off. "I still have the ones from the other investigations, thanks."

Dante took the card and slipped it into the inside pocket of his leather jacket. Loncar took down Dante's contact info and walked away.

"So now you have a choice," Dante said. "Let me take you home, or ignore the detective's request and drive yourself. What's it going to be, Samantha?"

15

AN UNDERSTANDING

Breakup Rule #5: Try not to repeat broken rules.

I woke up on the right side of the bed. The sheets were in a jumble, and Logan stared at me from the left.

"Don't judge," I said. "Detective Loncar had a bad night. I thought doing what he asked was the upright-citizen thing."

Logan meowed.

I rolled over and stared at the ceiling. This was the second time Dante and I had spent a night under the same roof. Exhaustion and injuries kept me from engaging in any hanky-panky, but judging from the state of the sheets, I'd either had a very restless night or I hadn't slept alone.

I couldn't help wondering what I was doing. It didn't feel like things were over with Nick. I closed my eyes, and Logan climbed onto my chest and lowered himself. He pushed his paws out in front of him, tickling the bottom of my chin. I turned my head to the left, and he stretched out more. One of his claws scraped my jaw.

"Ow!" I said. I rolled to my side, and he scooted off and

head-butted me. I freed a hand and ran it over his head, smoothing down the fur. He purred and curled himself into the nook created by my chest and my bent knees. I lowered my head to the pillowcase and rested my arm loosely around him. "You're being a very good cat through all of this," I said.

He lifted his head and opened one eye, blinked, and lay his head back down.

"I don't need Nick, and I don't need Dante, but I need you," I said, and kissed him between his ears. He purred.

I dozed off again, waking to the sound of knuckles rapping against the doorframe.

"Rise and shine, sleepyhead," Dante said.

"What time is it?"

"Nine thirty."

I sat up in bed and immediately pulled the covers up to my chest when I realized I wasn't wearing a bra under my pajamas. Dante smiled. "I'll go out for coffee while you get dressed. It's going to be a busy day."

I waited until I heard the front door close and the car engine start. I re-dressed in the sweater and jeans from last night and went to the kitchen. I ate a piece of cold pizza left over from Brothers.

A strange sound came from the living room. It was the VCR I'd had since college, and I only used it when I found something that was important enough to tape. It sounded like it might be dying a slow death. I hit the eject button, and a tape popped out. And I remembered what I had thought important enough to tape: the local cable channel that had planned to broadcast Amanda's runway show.

Not being skilled in the art of video enhancement, duplication, or transfer, pretty much the only thing I could do with the tape was watch it. I rewound the brittle twenty-year-old tape and crossed my fingers that it would stay in viewable condition long enough for me to check it out. I pressed play.

The cable company hadn't made much of an effort for Amanda. A camera had been set up at the end of the runway. I picked out Dante and me on the left side of the screen, and after scanning the rest of the patrons, I found Clive on the right. Twenty-seven seconds in, I saw a man in a pork pie hat slip past the crowd and duck backstage.

Santangelo Toma. Despite his very public refusal of the comped tickets he'd been offered prior to the show, he attended. Which meant he'd been there, and his actions suggested an alibi.

When the lights dimmed and the loud Japanese pop music started, everything dissolved in darkness except for the runway. The graphics from the Godzilla movie were projected on the backdrop right above Amanda's name, and the first model walked out. She wore the China-chop wig that faded from red roots to orange to yellow ends, and she was dressed in the silver leather motorcycle jacket over a red pantsuit. She posed at the end of the runway and turned. The intricate embroidery I remembered on the back of her jacket was distorted by the grainy quality of the video.

Five models walked the runway before Harper appeared. Her wig was silver. The sleeves on her kimono dragged on the ground as she walked. I freeze-framed the video and stared at her face. Gone was the shy, nervous model who had asked for my help earlier. She looked confident, like she had a secret.

From this angle I didn't see the smoke behind her like I had at the live showing. I watched her work the kimono, and then it went up in flames. Someone in the audience screamed. The music was cut, and the house lights turned on. Harper struggled to get the kimono off. Nick appeared and tore it from her shoulders, and she ran backstage. The kimono was left in a burning heap on the runway. The fire caught onto the trail of rose petals. Seconds later, the fire was everywhere: walls, ceiling, chairs, backdrop. Guests fled from their seats. Someone knocked the camera over, and the video went to fuzz.

The early reports on the news hadn't shown any footage from the show, but if I was watching this much, then certainly Gigger and company had seen it too. I kept watching, hoping the image would return. Within seconds the screen defaulted to color bars, and then a message that said the programming had been interrupted. The counter on the VCR continued to advance, so I knew I'd gotten everything the cable channel had filmed.

Rewind. Watch again. Rewind. Fiddle with the remote. Zoom. Rewind. After close scrutiny of the crowd, I picked out Eddie and a few others from Tradava. I never saw Tiny or Amanda, but it made sense that they were both backstage, where I would have been if I hadn't been let go the night before the show.

I sat up straight. Nobody who worked at the show had been attacked. Not prior to me, not after me. Only me. Maybe the plan all along had been to set fire to Harper's kimono, and the warning was meant to keep me from paying too much attention to what had been going on.

I thought back to the day Harper had come to me about the ill-fitting garment. The sleeves had been long enough to drag on the ground, but when I'd first inquired about the need for alterations, Oscar had dismissed us, saying that

Harper had specifically been chosen to wear that kimono. Now I knew why. Someone had planned for her kimono to catch fire. I interfered with that plan when Harper came to me and I ultimately went to Amanda. But Amanda couldn't be the one responsible for destroying her own show. It didn't fit. Which took me back to motivation. To create a stir? To gain publicity? To destroy the show? Or to get Harper?

I dug my cell phone out of my handbag, tapped the screen to cue up my contacts, and flipped to the Fs. Under Fuzz, I found the detective's number. I called.

"Loncar," he said.

"Detective, this is Samantha Kidd." I waited a beat then forged ahead. "I've been reviewing footage of the runway show, and I had a couple of questions."

"When you say you were reviewing footage of the runway show, what exactly do you mean?" he asked.

"I set my VCR up to record the show." The phone went silent, and I imagined Loncar cursing the day my parents put the house up for sale. "I figure you've seen this same footage. Maybe it would help to bounce theories off each other? Since we're practically working together on this. I feel like we have an understanding."

"You might be confused about that."

"Did you check out the report of my attack?"

"Yes."

"Then you know I'm the victim here. I'm just trying to figure out who assaulted me."

"What are your questions?"

"Was anybody hurt in the fire?"

"No."

"Do you know how the fire was started?"

"We're working on that."

"Do you have any suspects?"

"Ms. Kidd, I think we've tapped out the limits of our understanding."

"Wait!" I paused for a second. "Are you still there?"

"Yes."

"The way I see it, this has to do with either Amanda Ries, the designer, or Harper, the model who was wearing the kimono. For all I know, I wasn't even supposed to be the target of the attack. I think I was at the wrong place at the wrong time."

"How do you figure that?"

"If it was about me, there would have been a second attack. I left the hospital and attended the show as a guest. I wasn't a threat from out front. Since I left the show, I've visited Amanda, gone to the crime scene, and gone home. If someone was after me, they would have had ample opportunity to get me. Which means whoever attacked me accomplished what they set out to do."

"Where were you when you were attacked?"

"I was on my way to my car. I was backstage, and then I walked past the food table to the exit. Nobody else was attacked, and nobody claims to have seen anything."

"Is that all you got?"

I thought back to the fitting. "There's something else. Harper—she's the model in the kimono. Have you talked to her?"

"We can't reach her. She's out of the country."

"Still? Isn't that suspicious? That in the middle of the fire and the chaos, she managed to get out of there, get to an airport, and get to Mexico?"

"I'm not at liberty to comment on Ms. Ashton's role in the investigation."

"What about the kimono? Harper complained about the fit. Amanda specifically picked that garment for her. Do you have somebody at the lab analyzing it for clues?"

"Ms. Kidd, this is not a TV show. Besides, the samples were destroyed in the fire."

"Was anything else damaged?"

"We're looking at claims from Warehouse Five, the makeup people, and the designer. If we can't link this crime to someone, Ms. Ries is going to pay out a pretty penny in insurance."

"Did anybody else lose property? Amanda's show was in the main hall of the warehouse, but other artists show their work there. What about them?"

"Outside of the fashion show, everything went untouched. If damages were sustained to anybody else on the property, they haven't been filed."

16

FORWARD NOT BACKWARD

THE REST OF THE TENANTS OF WAREHOUSE FIVE HADN'T BEEN impacted by the fire, but Amanda was at risk of losing everything. I hadn't been expecting that. "Thank you, Detective."

"You're welcome, Ms. Kidd."

Three fires at the same location: the one that was part of my attack, the runway show, and now the dumpster. It had to mean something, but what? What exactly did I know? Not much.

Could Gigger be right that the movement I'd seen was a rat? I shuddered. No, if I suspected it was a rodent big enough to catch my attention across the parking lot, I never would have driven over to see it. Someone had been back there. Either the person who set the fire or the person in the dumpster. I shuddered again.

Gigger might have assumed that I'd seen a rat, but Dante believed me. It was that belief that kept me focused on finding the truth. Last night, we'd been a team. Not the bumbling Keystone Cops type, but two people focused on finding answers. Already I could see that, when it came to investigation, Dante knew what he was doing. The cover story with Amanda, the camera with the infrared film, the wariness when giving a statement to Gigger all illustrated that. I could learn from him.

Dante hadn't chided me for the way I'd handled the police. He didn't warn me away from danger. Ever since I'd found evidence that he had a whole other life, one that had started long before he and I met, I wondered what else there was to get to know about him. But even that bothered me too. Was he just another mystery that I wanted to solve? And once I saw him as a real person, not a dangerous semi-stranger, would the attraction dissipate?

I hoped I wasn't that shallow.

More and more, as questions about the fire and subsequently the job with Amanda came up, I questioned my involvement. There was a bigger personal issue here, one that transcended the investigation and the dangerous situations in the past. It was my ongoing need to find where I fit in.

Giving up my job at Bentley's New York and moving back to Ribbon had been an intentional move to help me figure that out, but being back in the house where I'd grown up had had an unexpected side effect of grounding me somewhere in my childhood. Here I was, over a year into that move, and no closer to finding answers.

I loved the city of Ribbon, with its pretzel factories and Pennsylvania Dutch restaurants. What I didn't love was feeling like I'd somehow reverted back in time. In my professional life as a buyer, I'd known what I was doing. I had confidence in my abilities. And even though I knew I'd chosen to leave that job behind, it seemed I'd lost something of me in the process—something I hadn't known was there.

I hummed the Japanese pop song from Amanda's soundtrack that I suspected would be stuck in my head indefinitely and made a long-overdue phone call. Dante returned with the coffee a few minutes after I hung up.

"What were your plans for developing that film?" I asked.

"I'd like to get to it today, but first I need a darkroom."

"Take me to the crime scene so I can get my car. You can come back here. There's a small room in the basement where my dad used to make wine. I'll give you the keys, and you can do whatever you need to do to set it up as your darkroom."

"What are you going to be doing?"

"I have some personal business to attend to."

Dante didn't pry. I respected him a little more because of that. And even if he did ask, I wasn't sure I'd tell him where I was going.

Back to Bentley's New York to talk to my former boss. Because a year was long enough to flounder while trying to figure things out on my own. Life didn't seem to be headed the right direction, and there was a very small chance that I'd need to give up everything I thought I wanted in Ribbon and go back to the life I'd left behind.

After we retrieved my car from Warehouse Five, Dante followed me back to my house. I showed him the darkroom and left him alone while I showered and changed into a black leather skirt, black tights, and black over-the-knee boots. I pulled on a red motorcycle jacket, grabbed my keys, and took off.

Two and a half hours later, I pulled into a public parking

lot across from Bentley's New York and spent more on parking than I had on a pizza last night. The air was pungent with the mixture of Chinese food and cigarette smoke. I held my breath and jogged to the customer entrance on Broadway. Once inside, a determined perfume sampler added a spritz of the latest Estée Lauder fragrance to the olfactory mix.

Good times.

As if an autopilot program had been activated, I bypassed displays of new merchandise and hopped into the up elevator. When I reached the fourteenth floor, I got out, climbed three steps, followed a long hallway, and turned left. My former boss's office was the third on the right.

"Knock, knock," I said, lightly rapping my knuckles against the nameplate that read Marcia Dann. Marcia looked up from her computer and smiled.

"Well, hello, stranger," she said. "Come on in."

"Do you mind if I shut the door?" I asked.

"Go right ahead." She didn't seem surprised that I'd asked. "How's life in the small town?"

"I've found the simple life not so simple." I smiled. "It would appear I'm having a hard time transitioning from being a city mouse."

"Personally or professionally?"

"Both."

"Have you talked to your parents about this?"

"My parents told me to sell the house and move in with them until I figure things out."

"You're not moving in with your parents. Life is about moving forward, not backward."

"I guess that means you don't think I should ask for my old job back?"

She leaned back and tapped a soft pink sculptured nail on her desk. "You could have asked me that question over the phone. What's the real reason you drove a hundred and fifty miles to see me?"

I collected my thoughts for a few seconds while fragmented memories of my nine years at Bentley's filtered through my mind. "You took a chance on hiring me, and I learned more working for you than any other time in my life —at least until I moved back to Ribbon."

"Yes, I imagine three homicide investigations can do that to a person." She smiled. "Samantha, do you remember the year I hired you?"

I nodded.

"You didn't know everything there was to know about being a buyer. In fact, you didn't know much about being a buyer at all. But you had a certain skill set: creative and analytical. You watched the other buyers. And you learned fast. By the time you resigned, you were the person other buyers watched."

"It's just that, now, something is holding me back. The job at Tradava didn't work out, and then the job at Heist didn't last, and, well, something's got to give."

"You wanted to leave Bentley's. Coming back here isn't going to give you any satisfaction. You thrive when there are problems to be solved. You already know how to solve the problems of retail. Three-month projections, overstocked inventory, assorting a department, making advertising choices. You need to apply that same analytical thinking that served you as a buyer to your own life."

"Do you think it's that easy?"

"Nothing good in life is easy. But people do things so they can grow. If you haven't grown from this move, then you haven't figured out why you went there to begin with." She leaned back. "Let me ask you this: why did you want to work at Tradava?"

"I was in Ribbon, my parents were moving, and Patrick found me sitting in the parking lot with my cat. We talked for five minutes, and we clicked. It felt like a sign."

"Patrick was a genius, and he would have made a good mentor, but you were overqualified for the job. If that had worked out, you would have been so bored you'd have asked for your old job back a year ago."

She slid the top drawer of her desk open and pulled out a red business card that said *Retrofit Magazine.* "A friend of mine is starting up her own magazine. She's looking for a fashion director, someone who can recognize trends and work independently. We're not talking comfortable little job here, Samantha. We're talking international travel for Fashion Week. Discovering new talent. Getting in on the ground floor of something new." She tapped the card on the desk. "You could do this if you wanted."

She held out the card. This was it. This was the opportunity I wanted.

I took the card. "Thank you, Marcia," I said.

She held her hands up. "Don't thank me. I have no say on whether or not you get the job. There are probably a hundred fashion bloggers out there who would sell off half of their closet for this opportunity. If you want it, you're going to have to go for it. And I mean that literally—she's going to need to see what you can do."

"Anybody who would sell off half of their closet for this opportunity should rethink the clothes they've been hoarding all these years."

"That's why I'm giving you the card."

We caught up on industry gossip before she headed to a meeting, and I left. I had driven over two hours for a thirty-minute meeting that restored my self-confidence and recharged my core values. I left Bentley's feeling more inspired than I had twenty-four hours ago and more resolute that my decision to leave had been the right one.

It was a little after two. Traffic would become an issue by three, although there was no good time to drive in Manhattan. Still, I couldn't resist a quick trip to Figaro for an afternoon chocolate soufflé. It's important to recognize the special things in life. And it was right around the corner.

I walked to the corner of 57th and Broadway. Figaro was a small European restaurant nestled in the middle of an otherwise residential street. A chalkboard out front listed the specials. It was the only indication that an eatery resided below street level. The chocolate soufflés were legendary to those in the know and took twenty minutes to rise. The hostess led me to a window table, where I placed my order without looking at the menu.

Eleven minutes of staring out the window while waiting, I saw a familiar person walking down the opposite side of the street.

What was Nick doing in New York City?

He crossed to my side of the street. I picked up my handbag, coat, and scarf and asked the hostess where the restroom was. I gave him five minutes to get past Figaro before coming out.

When I left the restroom, he was being seated.

I glanced at my table. My soufflé sat, alone, next to my water glass. The soufflé was already starting to fall.

Crap. The only reason I knew about this restaurant was

because Nick and I used to have business dinners here during Market Week.

My options were limited. I ducked behind a ficus tree and leaned forward, flagging down the hostess. She didn't look at me until after I resorted to *"Psst!"*

"Can I help you?" she asked.

I kept my voice low. "I have to leave. That's my soufflé on the table over there." I pointed. Nick looked up, and I ducked behind the tree again. "Can I get it wrapped up to go?" I whispered.

"There's no way to transfer it from the clay pot to the takeout container. Plus, they have to be eaten right away," she said.

"Do what you can. It's an emergency." I pulled a twenty-dollar bill from my wallet and thrust it at her. "I'll be waiting outside."

The fallen soufflé was gone by the time I returned to Ribbon. I'd like to say it helped me feel better, but it didn't. The only thing it accomplished was making my skirt feel tight in the waist.

17

MEATLOAF

I PULLED INTO MY DRIVEWAY AT SIX THIRTY. MY SPONTANEOUS tell-me-why-I'm-fabulous trip had taken most of the day thanks to my chocolate soufflé-and-Nick surprise, but a particular clarity often follows a quenched chocolate craving. I'd been able to focus on the matters at hand while driving. And, as I'd come to organize them while sitting in traffic, the matters at hand were as follows:

1.Get job.

2.Find out who's out to get Amanda and why I was attacked in the process.

3.Buy Logan one of those As-Seen-on-TV cat toys.

4a. Analyze feelings about Nick and

4b. Determine how they pertain to feelings about Dante.

5.Start exercise regime!

During the last twenty minutes of traffic I'd taken time to rank them in order of importance.

I didn't know if I would be coming home to company or not. My self-confidence detour through New York had left me with a feeling of independence and purpose I'd sorely needed to find. I hadn't called Dante to check in. It wasn't until my car was safely parked in my garage that it occurred to me that he hadn't checked in with me either.

There was a note taped to the TV. *Samantha, photos are in the darkroom. I leave it up to you to review and share with your detective friend.*

I filled Logan's water dish and shook a few extra cat kibbles into his bowl. He buried his face in his food as soon as I set it down. I left him alone in the kitchen, figuring we'd have time to catch up later.

I jogged down the stairs and went into the darkroom. The room, originally designed to be little more than a large storage closet, was lined on the right with built-in counter tops that wrapped around to the back wall. Basins of liquid sat next to each other along the counter. Light bulbs were suspended above them from cords that were duct-taped to the wall to keep them out of the way.

The left-hand side of the small closet was filled with metal baker's racks that held cast-off games, toys, and empty glass bottles that my dad had at one time planned to use for his homemade beer and wine. An old scuba suit hung from the corner of one fixture. The mask, snorkel, and flippers sat in a pile on the floor.

I approached the right side of the room. Hanging above the basins of liquid was a length of twine, strung from wall to wall like a clothes line. Small black binder clips secured 8x10 photos of the crime scene onto the twine. I scanned the lot of them, wondering what, if anything, I'd notice.

I spotted the silver wig in the fourth picture. The wig Harper had worn.

The composition of the photo caught the corner of the warehouse. I glanced at the preceding photos and saw what

Dante had done. He had started with his back to the building and taken the first picture and then snapped additional pictures as he slowly turned around. In an aerial view of the lot, his pictures would make up one o'clock, three o'clock, nine, and eleven. The photo with the wig was at nine. The wig was on the ground next to a somewhat-rusted tin trash can.

Since being involved in a homicide when I first moved to Ribbon, I'd tried to make up for what I lacked in common sense when it came to crime scenes. I read *Forensics for Dummies* and watched *Adam-12* marathons when I was alone. It was no citizen's police academy, but it was something. It made me think that, if a crime had been committed at this warehouse days ago, the police would have searched through the trash to look for clues.

Which meant the trash overflowing from this can was new.

Which told me someone from the fashion show had returned to Warehouse Five after the fire and thrown the wig out.

What it didn't tell me was why.

I started back at the beginning and followed the narrative. They told a story that continued around the perimeter of the building to the other side of the lot where I'd been. A few photos included me, approaching the dumpster. The last one was me, turned around, yelling for Dante. After that, he must have let the camera dangle from his neck when he ran to where I was.

If I hadn't yelled for him, he might have crept closer. He might have photographed evidence of whatever—or whoever—I'd seen by the dumpster. He might have seen it too.

Whoever started the fire had taken a big chance in doing so while we were on the property. They could have been spotted. Either the fire had been for our benefit, or someone had been trying to destroy evidence before we discovered it. Had that someone been watching us the entire time we were there?

It would take a remote detonator to start a fire from a distance. How far of a distance? I didn't know. But assuming the arsonist had been watching me approach the dumpster, there was a chance he didn't know about Dante, who had been on the other side of the building. That meant the arsonist didn't know about the existence of the photos.

Suddenly, it seemed very important that I set up a meeting with Detective Loncar.

I unclipped the photos and carried them upstairs. The mailman had delivered my auto-insurance documents last week, and I slid them out of the envelope and replaced them with the pictures. I called Loncar. It was seven thirty, and I wondered briefly if his wife ever questioned his off-hour phone activity.

When he answered, I identified myself. "Detective Loncar, this is Samantha Kidd. I know you weren't expecting to hear from me, but I have some information I need to give you."

"Ms. Kidd, I'm about to sit down to dinner. Can this wait until tomorrow?"

"Okay, sure," I said. "I'll come to your office. What time?"

There was a pause. "What's this information in reference to?"

"The Warehouse Five explosion last night. I have pictures that I think you should see, unless you'd rather I take them to Inspector Gigger—"

"Where'd you get these pictures?"

There was no way to skirt the issue and expect the detective to take me seriously, but I didn't want to drag Dante into anything he shouldn't be a part of. "The pictures are legitimate. Anything more will have to wait until we meet."

He made a noise that might have been accompanied by a shake of the head or an eye roll. "Ms. Kidd, where are you?"

"At my house."

"Same address?"

"Same address."

"Hold on." I heard muffled sounds, as if he was holding his hand over the receiver. Seconds later he returned. "You planning on going out any time soon?"

"No."

"I'm on my way."

By the time Loncar arrived, I had the photos scattered around the living room. They started on the gray sofa and worked their way around the floor to the black-and-white armchairs that sat in front of the blue tweed curtains. The last few were on the chrome-and-glass coffee table, resting on top of the latest book on Halston. There was probably a more standard way to assemble them, but I wanted Loncar to see the photos in the same order I had.

"Hi, Detective. Come on in," I said after greeting him at the door.

He leaned into my house and looked around first and then wiped his feet on the Welcome mat and crossed the threshold.

The last time Detective Loncar had been inside of my house was the day he'd taken me to the police station for suspicion of murdering my boss. I liked to think we'd come a long way since then. Maybe I should have picked up some champagne to celebrate.

"I'm sorry to pull you away from your family time and your dinner."

"Don't mention it."

"No, this could probably have waited—"

"My wife made meatloaf. The last three times she made it, it was still raw in the middle. There's not enough ketchup in the world to save raw meatloaf."

Considering my culinary skills—or rather the lack thereof—I filed that bit of info away for future reference. Who knew ketchup was part of the meatloaf-serving process?

He looked at the photos strewn around the room. "So, what do you have?" he asked.

In the thirteen minutes after hanging up with Loncar and determining the layout of the photos, I convinced myself to tell him where the pictures had come from. I'd started looking into this whole thing because I'd been attacked, but after seeing a body part in the dumpster, I knew that attack was minor compared to whatever was going on.

"Remember the photographer I introduced you to last night? Dante Lestes?" Loncar nodded. "He took these pictures while we were there."

"You didn't mention these last night."

"Dante was on the other side of the warehouse. I didn't know what he was doing over there. He ran around to my side when I saw the fire—and the leg—and the—"

"Explosion. I remember your statement." He shoved his

hands into the pockets of his brown coat and looked at the layout of photos.

"Start here," I said, and led him to the first photo. I stood back and watched him move from one to the next, occasionally looking back. When he reached the photo of the trash can by the back door, he picked it up and looked at the back left corner.

"Look at the—"

He cut me off with a hand held palm-side out. I bit my bottom lip and waited for him to say something.

He pulled his cell phone out, thumbed the screen, and held it up to his head. "Yo, chief. Remember those photos from the fire at the warehouse last week? Uh-huh, uh-huh, uh-huh. Find me the one on the north side of the building and check if there was any trash in the bin. They did? Where's it now?"

I stepped forward and opened my eyes wide like I wanted him to tell me what was going on. He turned his back to me. "Uh-huh. Good. Yep. Tomorrow." He hung up.

"Ms. Kidd, tell me what made you notice this particular photo."

"Well, there shouldn't be any trash in the bin, right? Your guys would have emptied whatever was in there the day after the fire. Why's it full? I could understand maybe a couple of paper cups or something, but full? That tells me someone was there after the fire. Someone who had enough to throw out that they filled that trash can."

He nodded.

"And then there's the wig," I added.

"The wig?"

"Right there, that silver thing on the ground. That's the wig Harper Ashton wore in the fashion show the night of the fire. What's it doing in the trash now? Why wasn't it there two days ago? Who threw it away?"

"You're sure Harper wore the silver wig?"

"Yes. I was there. I saw it. Detective, I think somebody's been back to Warehouse Five. I think last night's fire was about destroying evidence."

He picked up the photos from the black-and-white chair closest to the door and sank into it. "Ms. Kidd, we looked in the dumpster after you left last night. We didn't find evidence of a body. The dumpster contents were pretty much destroyed by the time the fire was out, and without a body, there's no homicide. There's no investigation."

"You think I'm making all of this up?"

"No." He set the stack of photos on the coffee table. "We did find one thing on the ground by the edge of the property."

"What?"

"A key card to the warehouse. Photo ID on it says it belongs to Santangelo Toma."

18

MAGNET FOR TROUBLE

"SANTANGELO TOMA IS AN ARTIST WHO RENTS SPACE INSIDE Warehouse Five," I said.

"What else do you know about him?" Detective Loncar asked.

"Just that he didn't like how Amanda's team took over the warehouse. He said he hadn't been able to concentrate since they started setting everything up, and he couldn't wait until the show was over. He called it a circus and was unhappy about the whole thing."

Loncar leaned forward. "How unhappy? Are we talking annoyed or angry?"

"He filed a complaint with the building management, but they ignored him. The money Amanda's show was expected to pull in far outweighed the rent of any of the other tenants, so his complaints fell on deaf ears."

"Was he the only one who complained?"

"I think so. He said he started a petition to get her kicked out of the warehouse, but nobody wanted to sign it. Tiny arranged for the rest of the tenants to see the show. Ribbon isn't the biggest town in the world, and most of them were excited about the idea that a major fashion show was going to take place where they worked."

"She excluded him?"

"No, he tore up the tickets and threw them back at her. But he was there. I saw him go backstage before the show. It's on the video. Do you want to see?"

Detective Loncar glanced at my ancient VCR. "I've got my own copy. Thanks." He picked up the stack of photos and tapped the edge along the glass coffee table. "Did you have any personal beef with Mr. Toma?"

"Not that I'm aware of. Do you think he was burning a body in the dumpster?" I shuddered.

"Ms. Kidd, The human body is 90 percent water. It's very difficult to cremate one in an open fire. If there was a body in there, which I'm not saying there was, it wouldn't have burned through all the way."

"What are you saying?"

"It's highly unlikely that what you saw was a human body."

I sat on the arm of the sofa where Logan had been sitting. He sprung out of my way to the back and walked along the top of the cushions like it was a catwalk. Which, considering he was a cat, it was.

"Ms. Kidd, is there anything else you want to tell me?"

"Like what?"

"I'm not the lead on this investigation. Inspector Gigger is. He's taken over everything that we've found and cut us out of the loop. His goal is to find the arsonist. Your statement made it seem like there might have been a murder vic in the dumpster, but we found no evidence of that. Our clues either went up in smoke or were washed down a sewer drain by the firefighters. If you got a theory, I'm willing to listen."

I turned my head and looked at Logan. He was in a ball, his fur spiking up and back. He watched Loncar out of the corner of his eyes, like he knew this man wasn't a regular visitor to our house. I turned my attention from Logan to the detective and saw him watching my cat too.

"Black cats aren't bad luck," I said.

"I know. I have three of them."

As if that was what he needed to hear, Logan stood up and skulked across the length of the sofa, down the arm, to the floor. He sat six inches from the sole of the detective's boot and started to clean his private parts.

"I think whoever started last night's fire was trying to destroy something. Even if he saw me, he might not have known Dante was on the other side of the building. That might be the movement I saw: someone setting fire to the bin. When I went over to investigate, he took off. You just said if it wasn't for me, you wouldn't have even known about that fire."

"You keep saying 'he.' I'm not convinced that the presence of Mr. Toma's ID means he's the arsonist. You got any reason to think it's a man?"

"No. The person who attacked me could have been a man. And I don't mean to sound sexist, but starting fires just seems like more of a man thing. You know, from the caveman days."

He smiled and then tried, too late, to stifle it. "For someone who pulls this stuff out of thin air, you're not too far off. Most arsonists are men. But until we figure out why he's setting these fires, there's not much more a profiler can do."

"I have a theory on that too," I said, bolstered by his compliment. "If this were a serial arsonist—someone who gets their kicks by scaring people—he wouldn't target Amanda, would he? But so far, I was attacked in that parking lot, Amanda's runway show went up in flames, and now a fire was started behind the warehouse. It seems like too much coincidence to be random."

"You think this is someone with a bone to pick with Ms. Ries?"

"She did get those threatening letters," I said.

"You mentioned these letters once before. Tell me about them."

"Come on, Detective, you knew about them before I did."

"Humor me."

"Fine. Two days ago, I went to Amanda's studio. I didn't plan to go there, and I can't say why I went there, but I did. After her partner left, she showed me the letters. There were six of them. Threats. Someone had been trying to scare her before the show. 'Burn, baby, burn,' 'All's well that burns well,' 'If you can't stand the heat, get off the runway.' Stuff like that. They were made from letters cut out of fashion magazines."

"How do you know that?"

"Give me some credit. I can recognize the B in 'Harper's Bazaar' from twenty feet."

He sat up and stared at me while I talked. "Where are these letters now?"

"I figured your department had the originals. I saw copies. I don't know where the copies are now, but there's a chance that Oscar LeVay took them from Amanda's desk."

Loncar stood up and walked away from me. He pulled

his phone out and made another call, his voice low and hard to understand. I heard "Ms. Ries" and "letters" and "last week." Then a series of "uh-huhs," a "yeah," and a "got it." He hung up and shoved his phone back into his pocket before turning back around. He sat in the chair opposite me and leaned forward.

"Guy at the desk remembers Ms. Ries coming in last week. She asked what we would do if we found out someone was threatening her. She didn't mention the letters, but the timing fits."

"What did your guy tell her?"

"The truth. The problem with threats is we can't act on them. If we get a chance, we can keep an eye out for suspicious behavior, but other than that, we're stuck until a crime is committed."

"You're saying I could put threatening notes in my neighbor's mailbox—"

Loncar held up his hand. "Putting something in a mailbox is a federal offense."

"Humor me. I could leave her nasty notes to say I was out to get her, and even if she knew the notes were from me, you couldn't do anything?"

"Do you have a beef with your neighbor?"

"She doesn't have to spy on me so much, but other than that, we're good. So?"

"If you threatened your neighbor, and she came to us, there would be a record of her complaint, but unless you acted on that threat, there's not much we can do."

"In Amanda's case, first she was threatened, and then I was attacked. Wasn't that enough?"

He leaned back. His shirt was unbuttoned at the neck and his tie was slightly askew, as if he'd thrown it back on before he came to my house. One of these days I was going to set Detective Loncar up with a personal shopper, just to see what would happen if he dressed in clothes that fit.

"Here's how it goes. Ms. Ries comes to the station and tells the desk sergeant somebody's been threatening her. This isn't the first time she's been at the center of a scandal, and this time she has a runway show coming up. Could be a ploy for publicity. But she's a pretty lady, and she seemed scared, so the desk sergeant answers her questions and tells her to come back when something happens."

"Right. But what about me?"

"See, that's a problem too. Your attack wasn't connected with Ms. Ries. You were assaulted in a public area. You were hospitalized. The report on you went to a different division. Assault charges by unknown assailant. A couple of the beat cops took that report and filed it."

"You checked it out?"

He nodded. "Then there's this fire at Ms. Ries's show. Now Gigger gets called in. His job is to find out who set the fire and stop him before he sets another one. Arsonists prey on people's fears. Even without a murder, you're looking at a lot of heat on the precinct."

"And you were shut out of the investigation. But if—"

"If there had been a body last night, I'd be looking at a homicide investigation. Instead, everything about this case has been departmentalized. I'm looking at a fraction of the big picture. And Gigger's not the sharing type. His one goal is to catch this arsonist before he strikes again."

He leaned back in his chair and smoothed his tie down to his ample belly. "Ms. Kidd, what's your interest in this? I don't mean to get too personal, but it never seemed to me like you and Ms. Ries were close friends."

"Somebody attacked me. Maybe everybody else is willing to dismiss it, but I'm not."

"Most people would take some time to recover, maybe get out of town for a few days."

"I'm not most people."

"Yeah, I figured that out already."

"Detective, I know you think I'm a nuisance. Somebody who showed up in your backyard and has been in the middle of three of your investigations. You might even call me a magnet for trouble, but you'd be wrong. All of this trouble, it was here before I ever came back to Ribbon. I checked. This city's crime has been on the rise for the past decade. I moved here because I had fond memories of the city where I grew up, but the city I'm living in now isn't the one I remember."

Loncar's expression changed. His eyes narrowed slightly, and his lips pursed, like he was considering how far he'd let me insult the city he was charged with protecting. Only thing was, it was my city now too.

"How long have you lived here?" I asked.

His head tipped to the side. He didn't answer right away. Logan stood up and walked past him, rubbing his back against the detective's pant leg.

"I was in Harrisburg five years ago. Picked up a lead on a trail that had gone cold. Couple of kids broke into a row home in center city and killed a man for kicks. I never saw anything like that." He shook his head. "Punks wrote messages on the walls in the victim's blood."

"Like *The Shining*," I said.

"Yeah, only they couldn't spell. The walls looked like something those Chick-fil-A cows might have written.

Woulda been a joke if it hadn't been real. That's when it hit home that bad people weren't restricted to big cities."

"That's when you transferred to Ribbon?"

"Yep. Moved when the transfer came through."

"And crime's been on the rise ever since?"

"Yep."

"Maybe *you're* the magnet for trouble," I said.

Loncar smiled.

"Detective, you wanted to know my interest in this. Here it is. I moved back here so I could figure out a more satisfying life for myself. New York City is great for a lot of people, but it wasn't right for me. But since I've been back, I've been framed for murder and almost killed. I volunteered at the exhibit at the museum because I thought it would lead to a job opportunity, but we both know how that turned out. The only job with any security was the one I worked when you asked me to rat on my employers. I'm not trying to prove anything to anybody but myself."

He ran his palms down the thighs of his trousers twice and then rested his hands on his knees. "About that. You got a knack for figuring things out. Now normally, I wouldn't want to encourage you, but it seems I owe you one. You surprised me by showing me these photos. Gigger doesn't have these photos." He held his hand up to keep me from interjecting. "I'm going to share them with him, because that's how this works. But I appreciate you calling and not just because you got me out of meatloaf."

"I'd offer you something to eat, but I don't cook," I said.

"That doesn't surprise me."

"I could if I wanted to. I just have other priorities, that's all."

He stood up. "Ms. Kidd, I'm going to ask you for a favor."

The hair on the back of my neck stood up.

"If you find out anything else that you think relates to any of this, you call me. Deal?"

"That's your favor?"

"I'm not asking you to look for evidence. I'm asking for you to call me if you think you figured something out."

In that one moment, something shifted. I knew it, and Loncar must have known it, but we both acted like everything was the same.

"Sure," I said. He turned to leave, and I followed him to the door. He was halfway to his car before I called out after him. "Hey, Detective?" He turned around. "I think this is the beginning of a beautiful friendship."

"I had a feeling you were going to say something like that," he grumbled. He got into his car and drove away.

19

OPPORTUNITY KNOCKING

THE FIRST THING I DID WHEN I WOKE UP ON TUESDAY morning was to find the business card for *Retrofit Magazine*. I propped it on the kitchen counter, filled Logan's bowls, and brewed a pot of coffee. I didn't feel my professional self until I showered and dressed, which was eight thirty. I finished off a cup of coffee and called Eddie at Tradava.

"Yo," he answered.

"In thirty seconds or less, can you tell me what's so great about me?"

"Why? You didn't buy purple hair dye, did you?"

"No! I—I'm going for a job today. A bonafide job that isn't working for someone I know and isn't—hopefully—connected to any sociopathic business people."

"You're serious?"

"As a heart attack," I said.

"Dude, it's about time." He paused for a second. "Okay, highlights: you know seven ways to tie an Hermes scarf. You can get ready in fourteen minutes. You are the only woman I know who can wear a necktie and not look butch. And you can eat an entire order of onion rings yourself."

"Those are the highlights?"

"Ask another guy, get another answer."

"Fine. What are my weaknesses?"

"There's no polite way to answer that."

"It's an interview question. She's going to ask. What are my weaknesses?"

"You're incapable of seeing your faults."

"Ha, ha."

"What do you want? You're a Taurus. You're stubborn, self-indulgent, materialistic, and possessive."

"I'm not feeling so good about the onion ring thing anymore."

"Dude. We work in fashion. Of course you're materialistic. And the self-indulgent part? It could be a lot worse."

"What about possessive?"

"Let's just say you still call the trend-specialist job at Tradava yours, and it's been, like, over a year."

"Do you think I can't move on?"

"Here comes the stubborn thing. You think I'm telling you that you can't move on. Now you're going to move on to prove to me that you can. But when you get down to it, I just want you to find whatever it is that's going to make you happy."

"What if what makes me happy takes me back to New York?"

"What can I say? I'm a Gemini. I want everybody to be happy."

"Okay, thanks. I have to go put on shoes and make this phone call."

"You can make a phone call in your bare feet."

"Not if I want the job, I can't."

"Dude." He hung up.

It was two minutes to nine when I called Nancie Townsend. This time she answered.

"Nancie, hi, this is Samantha Kidd. I'm calling about the job at *Retrofit*. Marcia Dann from Bentley's New York sent me. Not sent me. Told me. About you. About the job. I'm it. I'm your gal. I can finish an entire order of onion rings in one sitting."

Did I say that?

Nancie cleared her throat. "Samantha Kidd. You worked at Bentley's New York? For how long?"

"I was with Bentley's for nine years."

"Experience at a major New York luxe retailer. That's perfection."

We spent the next twenty minutes on the phone, talking about orange being the new pink and green being great for food with 30 percent less fat and awful for magazine covers. She laughed at my joke about culottes making a comeback and wanted to know what I thought about country-western as an emerging trend. I said something about suede fringes being acceptable for five minutes every ten years, and she didn't hang up. Things were going well.

I knew what was coming. I knew the inevitable "where are you working now?" question was on the horizon. And aside from a rundown of the dead ends I'd had over the past year, there was no way to distract her, so I headed her off at the pass.

"Nancie, here's the thing. I want this job. I'm qualified for this job. I've had a spotty work history since leaving Bentley's, but I've managed to keep myself connected to the fashion industry. As a matter of fact," I said, my self-indulgent Taurus side directing me, "I've been working with Amanda Ries recently. Her name has been in the news a lot lately."

"I've seen the coverage. That's one heck of a story. From what I saw, the clothes were amazing. Could you get an exclusive?"

"Let me ask her. She's been open to a lot of my suggestions," I exaggerated.

Big mistake. Huge.

"Perfection! Get me an exposé, something about Amanda's troubles. I want it all. The struggles, the collection, the fire. Oh—this will be fabulous. I can see a regular feature: 'designers in the hot seat.' Backstage with designers who are about to have a make-it-or-break-it show. How soon can you get it to me?"

I chewed my bottom lip and turned my back on Logan, who looked suspiciously like he was judging me. "Nancie, you do know that there have been more incidents since her show, right? Maybe instead of focusing on the fire, it's best to let the police find some answers."

"The police? As in, the fashion police?"

"No, as in the police-police. Men with badges who carry guns."

Her voice dropped to a whisper. "Do you know these men? Could we could do an article about them?"

"These police aren't the kind you'd want to feature in a fashion magazine," I said as an image of Gigger as Ichabod Crane popped into my head. "But I tell you what. I'll write a story about Amanda—about the collection and what it was like behind the scenes of the runway show—and email it to you."

"Perfection. But I want film, and I want it to be good. Have the article—with pictures—in my inbox by Friday morning. If it's good, I'll pay you freelance rates to run it, and you'll be the frontrunner for the job."

"Deal."

I took down her email address, and we said goodbye. I turned around to face Logan. "If you didn't like expensive cat food, I wouldn't have to worry so much about things like paychecks and jobs."

He stuck his paw in the air and swatted at a piece of lint and then turned around and disappeared through the narrow opening to the basement.

Now you've done it, I thought to myself. You leveraged your connection to your ex-boyfriend's maybe-former girlfriend's arson-tainted collection for a possible job opportunity.

One of these days I was going to take the easy road.

Okay, fine. Write an article about Amanda's show. I could do that. I'd spent time working backstage prior to the incident. I knew firsthand what went on before the show started, and I bet a lot of people would find that interesting. Forget the attack. Forget the fire. Forget the mysterious leg sticking out of the dumpster.

I shivered. None of that was going to be easy.

And on top of everything else, I'd promised Nancie photos.

First, I pulled a carton of Neapolitan ice cream out of the freezer. It was slightly less than half full. I ate a scoop and called Amanda. Tiny answered.

"Hi, Tiny. This is Samantha."

"Sam, hey. It's been a couple of days. How are you feeling?"

I cringed. I did prefer 'Samantha.' "Better. The first couple of days were painful, but the doctors said I'll heal. Thanks for asking," I added.

"The doctors gave you a clean bill of health? Which doctors? I'll follow up with them."

I misunderstood her. "I didn't accrue any major medical bills, but thanks for the offer." The phone was silent. "Tiny?" I prompted.

She laughed. "Medical bills. That's funny." She cleared her throat, and I realized the laughter had been forced for impact. "You were attacked in the parking lot. We don't carry liability insurance for accidents that take place in public areas."

"You thought I was going to sue you?"

"Just try it. I doubt you'll get far." There was an awkward pause. "Listen. Sorry about the accusations. Things have been tense around here ever since the fire. First your attack then the fire. It's a never-ending stream of bad publicity. I'd give my right arm for some good press right now."

"You can't honestly tell me that nobody from the media has contacted you about all of this. Somebody must have offered to run a puff piece in order to get an inside scoop."

"That's just it. I don't want a puff piece. I don't want the fire to be the focus. This is a business. Amanda needs coverage that's going to get us orders. Everything else is a distraction."

If I wasn't mistaking, that knocking sound I heard was opportunity standing at my door.

"Tiny, I might be able to help you with that. I spoke to a contact in the industry earlier today, and she's interested in a feature on Amanda's collection. Any chance you can talk her into giving me an exclusive?"

20

HAIL MARY

"WHAT'S THE FEATURE?" TINY ASKED.

"Backstage at a runway show, glamour of fashion, the hype of a new designer. That sort of thing."

"She could use something like that. Where will it be syndicated?"

"I can't say."

"Can't or won't?"

"Tiny, somebody's going to write about this sooner or later. Clive Barrington is bound to sell off his photos to the highest bidder. Amanda has a better chance of a fair story with me writing it than with a stranger. I can do the story based on my experiences prior to the show, but it'll be best if I write about the whole thing, fire and all."

I let my words dangle in the air for a few seconds. It was harder to not fill the silence with words than it was to sleep on my side with a midsection full of bruises. Finally, she spoke.

"Can you play ball with Clive?"

"If you give me his number."

She rattled off his digits, and I wrote them on the side of the ice cream carton.

"Be here in an hour. Oscar LeVay is coming for a meeting with Amanda. After that, you're up."

"See you soon." I hung up and grabbed my handbag. No way was I going to pass up a chance to watch Amanda interact with Oscar. I still suspected that he'd taken the threatening letters from her desk, and I wanted to know why.

I shrugged into my coat, wrapped a scarf around my neck, and whipped the front door open. Standing on my doorstep was Molly Diers, my sad-wardrobe client.

She wore the same olive-green snorkel coat she'd worn the first day we met. A brown stain had been added to the front. On her legs were heather-gray sweatpants that ended in elasticized cuffs right above thick white socks and neon cross trainers.

"I'm sorry I'm late," she said. "I had a last-minute yoga class this morning. Did I miss my whole appointment?"

In the mix of everything that had happened—the arson, the date-not-date with Dante, the trip to New York, the potential new job, and the visit with Detective Loncar—I'd completely forgotten about Molly's need for a makeover. The problem was, Molly was in need.

Really, really in need.

"I'm sorry you came all this way. Something came up, and I have to leave. It's an emergency."

"A fashion emergency? Bigger than me?"

I looked her over again. "Can you come back this afternoon?"

"The kids will be out of school at two forty-five. If I can come at four, I could focus more."

"Four. Sure." The only thing I had planned for the day was to go to Amanda's showroom and then come home and write an article for Nancie. I could do that in five hours, right? "Four o'clock. Meet me here, and we'll have another consultation."

"I don't need another consultation. I need clothes. I thought you were going to have something for me to look at today. My ex-husband is coming in for his parents' fiftieth anniversary, and he's bringing Lolita!"

"His new girlfriend's name is Lolita?"

"It might as well be. I can't see him like this." She looked down at the green snorkel coat and picked at a clump of what appeared to be dried-on scrambled eggs.

I did some mental calculation. Go to Amanda's, stop at Tradava on the way home to pick up clothes for Molly, and then come home and write the article. It would be tight, but I could do it. And in the category of keeping myself busy so I didn't think about Nick or Dante, it was just what the doctor would have ordered if there'd been a doctor in this scenario).

"I'll have everything ready when you get here."

"Great. Thank you, Samantha. You are a lifesaver," she said. She pulled a Kleenex from her pocket and dabbed at her nose. I wanted to spin her around and give her a push toward her car, but that seemed rude. Patiently, I stood on my porch and waited for her to put away the soiled Kleenex, pull flotsam out of her other pocket, and dig through it for her car keys. Two sourball candies wrapped in plastic and a pack of matches fell to the porch before she looped her finger through the key ring. I was afraid if she bent down to collect them she'd drop everything else in her hand.

"I'll get it," I said and stooped down. I closed a gloved

hand around the candies and picked up the plain white matchbook with my other hand. "Do you smoke?" I asked.

"No, why?"

"I don't see a lot of people with matchbooks these days."

"It's a memento. The last time a stranger hit on me in a bar."

I put my hand on her upper arm and gently turned her around. "Molly, things will get better for you. I don't know how long it's been, but you'll get back out there again."

"What do you mean?"

"I don't know how long you've been carrying around this packet of matches, but your confidence will come back. Before you know it, the nights when strangers hit on you will all run together."

She turned back to face me. "It was this past Saturday night," she said. She glanced at the matches. "He was a creep who was looking for a nude model. Do I look like model material?" She waved her hand up and down the length of her stained snorkel coat. "When my ex left me for a younger woman, I decided to teach my kids something about integrity. But please." She paused. "Do something about this." She left me on the porch and drove away.

I glanced down at the matchbook. It seemed silly that such a small thing could give Molly a confidence boost. It wasn't the matches themselves. It was what they represented.

I was about to toss them when I noticed something written on the inside. I flipped the package open and saw a phone number, followed by the letters C. B. I knew of a C. B. In fact, I knew of a C. B. who was just seedy enough to use a pickup line about models. I raced back inside and pulled the Neapolitan ice cream out of the freezer. The number I'd written on the side matched.

Clive Barrington had given away a pack of matches after the fire at Amanda's show. Did it mean something? I intended to find out. I called the number.

"Clive Barrington," he answered.

"This is Samantha Kidd."

"Ah, love, to what do I owe the pleasure?"

"I was talking to one of my clients, and she just so happened to have a pack of matches with your number on them." I paused for effect. "It struck me as curious that you had a pack of matches on you and that you gave them away the day after the fire at Amanda's show. Perhaps trying to rid yourself of evidence?"

"I hardly think I'd write my name and number inside matches that were used to start a fire. Come on, love. I expected more from you."

And I'd expected less of him. "She said you asked her to model for you. Is that the best pickup line you have?"

"I wouldn't resort to using something so mundane. The models I shoot aren't amateurs. Although I'd make an exception in your case. How about it, Ms. Kidd? Care to let me take artistic photographs of you?"

"No thanks." I hung up without saying goodbye. I tossed the matches on the counter and left.

Even with the sidetracks of Molly's appearance and the conversation with Clive, I still hoped to arrive at Amanda's before Oscar left. I'd have a better chance of getting film for my article if I showed up with a photographer than if I asked permission first. There was only one photographer I had a chance of getting on short notice.

"Dante, this is Samantha. Meet me at Amanda's

showroom as soon as you can. Bring your photography equipment." I left the address on his voicemail and disconnected. I nestled the phone into the cup holder next to the list I'd made yesterday while driving home from the Big Apple. "Get job" was at the top. *Stay focused, Samantha. This article is about getting paid, not about the investigation.* And if—no, *when*—I got the job, I'd celebrate by buying Logan that fancy cat toy. Productivity was my middle name.

I parked in the driveway next to a shiny black sedan. It was the same car that had parked next to the Corvette the first day I came to Amanda's studio. I followed the sidewalk to the front door and listened before knocking. The door was too thick. I bent down and crept under the front windows and then peered into the corner.

Oscar stood facing Amanda. Today he wore a navy blue three-piece suit with a paisley necktie. "Thank you for understanding," he said.

"Had she mentioned that she was going to Mexico?" Amanda asked.

"Harper was a loner. She didn't have friends at the agency. The only person she listened to was her sister. If anything, I'd think the others were jealous of her rise. Perhaps that made things more difficult for her. Perhaps that's why she left without telling anyone."

I strained to keep up with their conversation, plugging one finger into my right ear and pressing my left closer to the glass. The voices stopped. After a few seconds, the front door opened. Amanda looked at me standing under the window.

"You're early," she said.

"I was already on my way."

She leaned forward and looked at the patch of lawn

where I'd been standing and then turned around and went inside. I followed.

"Have a seat. Oscar and I are finishing up."

Oscar wasn't in the room, and I hardly suspected him of hiding behind the wicker screen like I'd done days before. "Where is he?" Just then, a toilet flushed. "Oh."

The tall man came out of the powder room. He saw me and then asked Amanda, "We've reached an understanding?" She nodded. He lifted a wool cape from a peg on the wall and draped it around his broad shoulders. He picked up his hat from a chair and tipped it my direction before putting it on and leaving.

"Is everything okay?" I asked.

"'Okay' is hardly the term I'd use."

"Is he still demanding payment?"

"Yes," she said. "And Tiny said I have to pay if I want to come out of this with my reputation intact."

"Where is Tiny? I expected her to be here."

"She's at the bank. Nobody wants anything from me except for money."

"Amanda, this article can help you with that. I don't know how much Tiny told you, but I saw the collection at the showroom. I know the vibe you were going for. I'm a good person to make this happen because of that. If you're interested, let me get a few shots around here. Your office, your inspiration boards, your samples. What didn't make the runway show and why? That sort of thing."

She sipped her coffee and the silence ballooned. I waited her out. Finally, she set the mug down on her desk and crossed her arms. "This collection was inspired by Kaiju movies and outer space."

"But prior to this collection, you were known for classic silhouettes. You interned for Maries Paulson—"

"Tiny doesn't want me to talk about that collaboration."

"Why not?"

"She says I have to make a name for myself, not rely on the names of people I worked for."

I didn't understand Tiny's motivation. Amanda's past collaborations and internships would separate her from a pack of recent design school graduates. Her experience would show that she had more than what you can teach in a classroom. Tiny sounded like she wanted to negate all of that. It seemed to me that Amanda didn't need a business partner. She needed a publicist.

"When you graduated from design school, your first solo collection was ice-cream factory meets Ralph Lauren. Lilac turtlenecks and riding pants, pink satin ball skirts with fitted T-shirts and cropped bouclé jackets, robin's-egg blue wool blazers with matching suede elbow patches. How do you go from that to Godzilla on the moon?" I waved my hand around the part of the showroom filled with racks of cast-off garments.

"My preppy stuff wasn't getting me noticed. Tiny said I needed a Hail Mary. That's what this collection was. A big risk that could have potentially changed everything. I had appointments with editors from all the major magazines lined up to view the samples after the show."

"What happens now?"

"No samples, no appointments." She waved toward a rack. "These are new. Tiny pushed me to make a second set of samples to show the buyers who showed interest." She stepped away from the fixture and looked over my shoulder. "Who are you?" she said suddenly.

I turned around. Dante stood inside the room.

"I'm the new photographer. Samantha asked me to meet her here." He pulled a business card from inside his leather jacket and handed it to her. She studied it for a couple of seconds and then stuffed it into her pocket.

"Tiny didn't say you were bringing a photographer," she said to me.

"Amanda, consider this a second chance to make that Hail-Mary pass that Tiny talked about. I'm here. He's here. We'll take photos. You can use them to shop the collection to whomever you want." I held my breath. Her eyes bounced back and forth between my left eye and my right, like she'd discovered that they were two different colors. (They weren't.)

"Your photographer isn't prepared for a full-on photo shoot."

"I have everything I need in the car," Dante said.

Now her eyes bounced back and forth between him and me. "You're not going to get a better chance than this one," I said. "Especially one that won't cost you an arm and a leg."

She pulled her phone out of her pocket and scrolled through her contacts. Before making a call, she looked up. "One model, one hour."

"I have a better idea," Dante said. "Let Samantha try on the samples. Save you money on a model and the time it would take her to get here. You'll be here the whole time, so you'll see everything I see."

Before I had a chance to point out that I wasn't exactly a model size, Dante pinched my arm. I didn't know him well enough to know what he was thinking, but I hoped he had more of a plan than embarrassing me with a split seam.

"That'll work," Amanda finally said.

"I'll get my equipment," he said. "Samantha, you want to help?"

"Samantha can get undressed. I'll help." She pointed to the small scrim that I'd hidden behind when Oscar LeVay had first stormed into the showroom. "Change behind that. Samples are on this rack. Considering the sizes, you might want to start with the kimonos."

I made a face at her behind her back and then, when the front door closed, grabbed a garment and disappeared behind the scrim. Within seconds my motorcycle jacket, sweater, skirt, tights, and boots were on the floor, and I was clothed in a thin red cotton robe. The showroom was colder than I would have liked, and as soon as Amanda and Dante returned, it would be obvious to everybody in the room.

While Dante's plan had the possibly intended goal of embarrassing me, it had also left me alone in Amanda's showroom until they returned.

First thing I did was look through her desk drawers for the threatening letters. With one hand holding the robe shut, I made slow progress. I needed both hands. I let go of the neckline and dug through her desk. Five pairs of scissors, a couple of tape measures, a stack of sketch pads. Paper clips, Post-its, pencils and pens and highlighters. I was so absorbed in the search of her desk that I didn't hear her come back inside.

"Just what the heck do you think you're doing?" Amanda asked.

21

BOW ON THE BACK

Breakup Rule #6: Keep wearing good underwear.

The red cotton robe flew open. Dante's camera snapped several shots. I pulled the robe closed and glared at him.

"I was looking for the letters," I said.

Amanda crossed the room and slammed her desk drawers shut. "You weren't supposed to tell anybody about those," she hissed. She looked at Dante and then back at me.

"I'm only trying to help."

"Then do what you said you were coming here to do." She disappeared into the back room.

Dante stepped closer to me. I looked up at him, my knuckles turning white as I clutched the robe shut. "Thanks for the heads up. I thought you were going to be lugging in a bunch of equipment?"

"I said 'equipment.' I never said 'a bunch.'" He glanced down at my white knuckles. "I know you're cold, but you're going to have to relax for the photos."

"Fine. Tell Amanda to turn up the heat."

He slipped his hand inside the collar of the robe, bent down, and kissed the side of my neck. Cold was no longer an issue.

I stepped back. "Let's do this."

One hour and seventeen costume changes later, I was back in my turtleneck, skirt, and boots. Dante had used one large overhead light as a spot above me. I rested in a chair opposite Amanda's desk while he packed it up.

"I'm curious," Amanda said. "Why do you use film when you could go digital?"

"Film captures reality," Dante said. "It takes more than a point-and-click mentality to get the shot. You know those Hollywood glamour photos from the thirties and forties? Film. One overhead light, just like we used here. The light defines the angles of the face. No need for retouching. You might want to consider it for your catalog."

"You're not going to touch these up?" I asked in a panic.

"I'll use a white pencil to bring out the highlights. I won't need more than that."

I found an empty hanger and rehung the red robe. It had served as my between-outfits costume, keeping the secret that I couldn't close most of Amanda's samples. Amanda glanced at me and stood up. "Can I talk to Samantha alone for a second?"

"Sure." I gave Dante an I-don't-know-what-this-is-about look. He hoisted his bag onto his shoulder, saluted us, and then left.

As soon as the door was shut, she held out her hand. "I'd like those letters back," she said.

"I don't have them."

"Where are they?"

"You left them on your desk the day you showed them to

me. I hid behind the screen when Oscar showed up, and when I came out, they were gone."

Her hand flew to her mouth. "Oscar took them? Why didn't you say anything?"

"I thought maybe you had the foresight to put them away before you let him in. If you didn't, then I think it's safe to assume he took them. You didn't think anything when they were missing?"

"Like I said, I thought you took them." Her eyes were wide with fear. "This is bad."

"Amanda, he only has a copy. Tell the police. They have the originals, right?"

"What are the police going to do?"

"They'll ask him about them. That'll keep you from being involved. Let Detective Loncar do his job," I finished.

Amanda shooed me out of her studio, and I found Dante waiting by the Corvette. "You were pretty good in there," he said.

"Yeah, well, don't do that to me again."

"What? I thought you'd like having a chance to examine the samples up close. I can't think of anything closer than getting you inside them."

"In case you didn't notice, I didn't entirely fit inside them," I said, remembering the strapless red gown that didn't zip up the back. Thanks to Dante's suggestion that I step in as a model, Amanda had gotten an unexpected peek at my underwear. Hard to maintain post-breakup moral high ground around the maybe-former girlfriend when she knows you have a bow on the back of your panties.

"Come on. I'll buy you lunch to make up for it."

"No thanks," I said. "I'm going to skip lunch. Too much

to do. You should get back to the darkroom to develop the film."

He slung his bag over one shoulder and tipped his head. "Just because the red gown didn't zip up over your hips doesn't mean you have to give up food," he said.

"You think the fact that I didn't fit in a sample-sized dress is going to make me give up food? You have a lot to learn about me."

"I guess I do."

I zipped up my coat. The air was cold and wet, like the gas around a fresh tray of ice cubes when you first pull them out of the freezer. I stopped by my car, closed my eyes, and took a deep breath. I held it in for a few seconds and then exhaled. The crispness invigorated me. I'd always loved the first cold snaps of the season, the promise of impending flurries, and the beauty of a fresh blanket of white snow when it covered the streets and yards.

A series of clicks sounded. I opened my eyes and found Dante aiming the camera at me. I threw my hand up in front of my face. "What are you doing? The photo shoot is over."

"Just thought I deserved something for my hard work."

"I think you got that something when my kimono opened up."

"I didn't look," he said. He kept a straight face, and I almost believed him.

I unlocked the car and tossed my bag on the passenger-side seat. "I have a client coming this afternoon, and I don't want any distractions."

"A distraction, huh? I was wondering how you compartmentalized me."

"I don't compartmentalize people," I said. Real classy, I

thought. That's the equivalent to did not/did too on the fourth-grade playground.

Dante folded his arms on the top of the Corvette and leaned on them. The black leather of his motorcycle jacket tightened around his muscles. A blast of wind tossed my hair around my face. Dante's jet-black Elvis-style hair barely moved, except for the strands that dusted his forehead.

"Samantha, I don't judge you for who you are, but that doesn't mean I don't see who you are. You put people in boxes to keep them separate from each other. It's like you're protecting your relationships so they're there when you need them. Friends go here." He stood up straight and pantomimed something on his left side. "Bad guys go here." He pantomimed to his right. "I don't know where you tried to file your last boyfriend. I don't even know if he's still in the picture." He walked around the Corvette and stopped when he was facing me. He reached a hand out and tugged on the collar of my coat. "I'm waiting to see where you file me."

"I can't offer you anything other than what we have right now," I said.

He picked up my hand and pressed my fingers to his lips. "You'll tell me when you figure things out?"

"I'll tell you when I figure things out."

He nodded and put his equipment in the Corvette. I got into my car, backed out of Amanda's driveway, and left. As I reached the corner, I glanced in the rearview mirror. Dante was still standing by the Corvette, watching me drive away. I turned right at the corner, turned right again at the stop sign, and pulled over into the red zone.

I wasn't anywhere close to figuring things out.

Since leaving Dante's apartment yesterday morning, I'd

gone to New York, reconnected with my boss, talked my way into a job opportunity, and established a working relationship with Detective Loncar. These were all people who served a purpose. Was Dante right? Did I compartmentalize the people in my life so they'd be there when I needed them?

I didn't like how that sounded. Even if, for the first time since leaving New York, I felt like I had something to focus on. If not for the arsons, things would have been looking good. Why? Because I'd pushed thoughts of Dante and of Nick out of my mind for twenty-four hours and focused on me? Or because I had temporarily surrounded myself with people who could offer me a boost when I sorely needed it?

That's it. I didn't want to be someone who used her friends. I thought back to Molly Diers's desperation this morning. She was counting on me to make things a little better when she had to face her ex and his new young girlfriend. I could do that. Starting now—right now—I was going to do something for someone else—for her.

Work history notwithstanding, Tradava was as good a place as any to start building Molly's new wardrobe. I went in a side door, past juniors, to the coffee counter. I found Eddie on the top rung of a six-foot-tall ladder, a hot glue gun in one hand and a fist full of glue sticks in the other.

As visual director for the store, Eddie oversaw the various displays that showcased designers, trends, and colors. Most people didn't recognize the effort that went into maintaining the newness of a store that had been around for several decades.

A row of white mannequins, clothed in ensembles of red, orange, and winter white, lined the wall usually occupied by a display of chocolates. I adopted a pose at the end of the row and stood still. Eddie climbed down the ladder and stood back, assessing the work he'd finished. He turned around and scanned the row of mannequins. When he got to me, he shook his head. Glue dribbled from the glue gun and left a trail down the side of his paint-stained jeans.

"If you're trying to get lost in a crowd, you might want to find a different crowd."

"You're saying I'm not mannequin material?" I asked. I put a hand on the arm of the mannequin next to me, and she rocked dangerously to the left.

"Dude!" Eddie said. He shoved the glue gun into his pocket, raced forward, and caught her. "These mannequins cost a grand a piece."

"For real?"

"New mannequins are either fiberglass or plastic, and they are the definition of cheap. I'm trying to maintain a tiny shred of nostalgia in an ever-changing world of hot pants and prom dresses."

Suddenly he hopped on his left foot and kicked his right foot like there was a mouse in his pant leg. He made a *woop woop woop* sound like Curly from the Three Stooges and hopped in a circle. The cord from the glue gun wrapped around his leg. Now tangled, he lost his balance and fell forward. His hands connected with the mannequin on the end and knocked her over. Her arm popped off, slid out of the sleeve, and landed on the ground. The plaster broke by her elbow, but the arm didn't fall off. I yanked the cord to the glue gun out of the wall.

"You're supposed to unplug it when it's not in use," I said. "Unless you know something I don't."

He picked up the plaster arm from the floor. There was a

half-inch space between the components that had broken, and in the middle was a steel rod.

"Another one bites the dust," he said.

"Why didn't it fall apart?"

"There's a steel frame inside the plaster."

"Can you shoot a bunch of hot glue in the middle and squeeze it shut?"

"I wish. When these old ones break, they have to be destroyed. There's too much chance of them cracking more and causing an accident around customers."

"You're going to send her off to the mannequin graveyard?"

"Worse. Broken mannequins have to be destroyed. Security arranges a pickup with a special trash-removal company. And I can't yell at anybody over this one because it was my fault." He suddenly looked at me. I held my hands up in front of my waist palm-side out.

"Don't even think about blaming this on me."

His shoulders fell, dejected. He pulled the large black radio off his belt. "Walt, this is Eddie. I got a broken mannequin on one, by the coffee shop. Nothing dangerous, but it's one of the old ones. It's gonna have to be burned."

My head snapped up. "Why do you have to burn it?"

He waved me silent and held the radio up to his mouth again. "Not the whole thing. Broken arm. Sure, I might have another lying around. I'll put it behind the coffee counter. Get it when you're ready." He hooked the radio back to his belt.

"Why do you have to burn them?"

"You see how big this thing is? Imagine how much space it would take up in the trash. And like I said, they're expensive. The iron framework inside can be recycled, but the plaster has to be burned off, and then the iron has to cool and be professionally cleaned before the company can start over. We get back like a tenth of the price of the mannequin, but it's something."

"Who burns them?"

"I don't know. Some company with a big incinerator. What do you care?"

I chewed on my lip and remembered the mannequins that were staged by the entrance of Amanda's show. "I have to call Detective Loncar. I think somebody might have been burning a mannequin in the dumpster behind Warehouse Five."

22

TOPEKA

BUT BEFORE I CALLED THE DETECTIVE, I NEEDED TO KNOW what I was talking about. "You said these mannequins were made of plaster. What else are they made of?" I asked Eddie.

"Horse hair and cotton fibers to make them stronger."

That's exactly what I'd started to suspect. I didn't know much about the flammability of plaster, but when you added in the content of cotton fibers, you had something that would burn. And if someone burned a plaster mannequin leg, the only thing left would be the steel rods inside.

I called Loncar. "Detective, remember how I saw a leg in the dumpster at Warehouse Five? But you found no evidence of a body? And how Ichabod—I mean, Inspector Gigger—didn't believe me?"

There was a sound on the other end of the phone like a chuckle.

"Gigger was right." I continued. "There wasn't a person in the dumpster. There was a mannequin. Maybe not a whole mannequin but a part of one. If you can come to my house tonight, we can go over my theory in more detail. I have an appointment at four that should last an hour, and that's my priority. And I have to write an article, but I can work on that after you leave. So, seven? Can you come then?"

"Fine," he repeated. "See you tonight."

———

MOLLY DIERS'S car was in my driveway when I returned home. I pulled in behind her minivan, backed out, and parked next to the mailbox. After wrestling with the merchandise I'd bought at Tradava after I called Loncar, I shut the door with my hip and headed toward the house. Molly was on my front porch with two boys. Logan sat inside the big picture window staring out, and one of the boys had his face pressed against the window staring in. The other boy sat on the swing next to Molly, his head buried in a book.

"I hope you don't mind. I was late picking the boys up from school and didn't have time to take them home." Her eyes cut to the packages draped over my arm. "Are those for me?"

"A couple of last-minute items," I said. "Why are you waiting outside? You must be freezing."

"They wouldn't stop bothering each other in the car. The rule was they could get out if they didn't talk."

I looked at the one with the book and the one antagonizing Logan. They looked angelic enough. If Molly could deal with her two boys sitting in the background while she tried on clothes, then I was going to deal with her two boys sitting in the background while she tried on clothes. I threw the bags over my left arm and unlocked the front door.

"Follow me," I said to Molly.

"Is she a witch?" the non-book-reading boy asked. "She has a black cat."

"She's not a witch, dummy," said the boy reading the book. "She's probably a pagan."

"Joseph!" Molly said. "You take that back."

"I take it back," Joseph said. "Maybe she *is* a witch."

I let Molly lead the way to my basement/studio and carried the shopping bags down the steps behind the trio. Not-Joseph sat on a folding chair, swinging his legs above the exposed cement floor. Joseph set his book down on the chair next to his brother and wandered to the bookcases against the back wall.

"Molly, are you sure you still want to do this today?" I asked.

"I told you this morning. I need a dress for this weekend, and I'm running out of time."

"But if you're busy keeping track of the boys—"

"Do you have any puzzles? They love puzzles. Any puzzles."

I scrounged around and came up with two unsolved Rubik's cubes. Within thirty seconds the only sound was the click of plastic against plastic.

First crisis averted.

"Today is about determining what shapes look good on you and what you like. We might not agree on everything. I'll give you an honest opinion, but ultimately it's your money, so you have to feel good about spending it," I said. It was the same speech I gave every client. I had a feeling Molly would take it more seriously than most.

"I can't believe this is my life. I used to know about stuff like this, and now I'm paying you to make sure I don't walk out of here looking like a fool," she said. "The things we do for family."

I hung the shopping bags on an empty rolling rack and tore the plastic down from the hangers. I handed the first round of clothes to Molly and lowered my voice.

"Remember those matches you dropped the other day? Is there anything else you can tell me about the guy who gave them to you?"

Her lips curled into a frown. "Why do you keep asking about him? He was a nobody."

"You kept the matches, which meant something,"

"Yeah, it meant I wanted to light some candles in my apartment." She grabbed the black dress in my hand and turned away.

"Molly, don't sell yourself short. You're a beautiful woman, and when we're done here, everybody is going to see it."

She looked at me for a second, and her expression softened. "He told me I reminded him of a model he used to work with," she said. "It was just a line that a creep in a bar probably uses on every woman who walks in, but I liked the way it sounded."

"It's the accent," I said. "Makes everything sound good."

"What accent?"

I narrowed my eyes and looked at her. Something didn't make sense. She took the clothes and undergarments that I held out to her and carried them to the darkroom I'd indicated for her fitting room. A moment later, the door opened back up, and she came out, her face bright red. Dante was behind her.

"I'm sorry," he said to Molly. "You surprised me as much as I surprised you."

Molly looked at him and then me. "Was that part of the plan—send me into a dark closet with a sexy man?"

"Nope. Not part of the plan." I glared at Dante and then turned back to face her. "This is Dante. He's a photographer. He sometimes uses that room to develop photos."

Behind me, Joseph spoke. "That's probably where she casts her spells."

"Mom! Don't go in there!" Not-Joseph cried out.

The look that I gave the two boys probably didn't do much to prove I wasn't a witch.

I turned back to Molly. "The room is empty now. You can go in and change."

She leaned into the doorway, more tentatively this time. When she was convinced no more tattooed bikers were lurking about inside, she closed the door behind her.

"What are you doing here?" I hissed at him.

"You told me to come here and develop the film, remember?"

"Are you finished?"

"The prints are drying. Who is this woman? Do you trust her? Because every photo I took today is hanging in there."

"She's a client." The door opened slowly, and Molly poked her head out. "Samantha, can I ask you something in private?"

I left Dante and crossed the room to her. "Yes?"

"These photos of you. What are they from?"

"I'm writing an article on a local designer and needed some art. Last-minute thing—no time to hire a model."

"That man is your photographer? Do you trust him?"

I looked at Dante, who was fiddling with one of the Rubik's cubes while the boys watched.

"More than I probably should," I said.

"I wish I met men I could trust." She shut the door again, and I went back to Dante.

"This woman just went through a nasty divorce. Her ex-husband has a girlfriend half his age, and her in-laws invited her and the kids to their golden anniversary party this weekend."

"I know you're not seriously leading up to asking me to be her date."

"God, no!" The clicking of the plastic toys in the background stopped. I froze and looked at Dante. He looked behind me. He smiled at them. The clicking started again. "If I'm going to help her, I need her undivided attention. That means no you and no them." I tipped my head toward Joseph and Not-Joseph. "As in, can you make them go away? Like, to the kitchen?"

"You think their mom is going to let me take her kids?"

"I think their mom would pay you to take her kids."

The door behind me opened, and I turned to look at Molly's head, poking out from behind the door. She looked nervous.

"Come on out," I said.

She walked to the center of the room wearing a close-fitting jersey wrap dress. Until today, I hadn't realized what kind of body Molly had under that snorkel coat. The jersey molded to her long, lean torso, nipping in at the waist where she'd cinched the wrap-around tie. Behind me, I heard the click of a shutter. Molly copped a couple of poses and pouted, and Dante clicked a few more frames.

"You're a natural," Dante said.

"It's the dress," Molly said. She stepped in front of the full-length mirror and studied herself.

"Molly, if it's okay with you, Dante can take the boys to the kitchen for a snack, and that'll give us a chance to concentrate."

"Yes, please," she said to Dante. He said something to the boys. They looked at him in awe. He tipped his head toward the stairs. "I hope you guys like ice cream and pretzels." He looked at me. I made a face. Not-Joseph giggled, and then the boys followed Dante.

"Who is he, the Pied Piper?" she asked.

"He's a friend."

"You think he's busy this Saturday night?"

"If I were you, I'd make other arrangements."

The impending in-law anniversary celebration had shifted Molly's priorities from single mother getting by to wardrobe overhaul. By the time we were finished, she chose two-thirds of what I'd assembled during my high-speed shopping trip at Tradava, including a paisley printed tunic, several pairs of boot-cut pants, an amber cowl-neck sweater with an asymmetric hem, two suede skirts, and the jersey wrap dress for the party. She wanted to pair it with fishnets and stilettos. Not entirely appropriate for a fifty-year wedding celebration, but if it was between that and her snorkel coat, I knew which way I'd cast my vote.

After Molly left with her boys in tow (freshly tattooed thanks to Dante's skills with a waterproof eyeliner pen), I opened and closed the cabinets looking for food. I wasn't known for going long stretches of time without a meal, and turning down Dante's lunch invite had left me hungry. And when I was hungry, I had a hard time focusing. I pulled a package of frozen chicken breasts out of the freezer and set them in the sink and then stared out the window into the yard next door.

"Topeka," Dante said, joining me in the kitchen.

"What?"

"Topeka. Capital of Kansas. The way you were staring out the window, I figured you were doing some mental gymnastics. For me, that's either state capitals or times tables."

"Why'd you say Topeka?"

"Most people get stuck on Kansas."

"I'm good with Kansas. I get lost in the M states."

He grinned. "The photos from today are in your basement. You want to go look at them? I didn't see anything abnormal, but I don't know what you're looking for."

"Sure." I went down the stairs with Dante behind me. The rack of clothes from Tradava stood in the middle of the basement, covered in cast-offs that Molly hadn't rehung. An ivory dress had fallen from the plastic hanger and lay in a pool of wool jersey on the floor. I tossed it over the top of the bar and then went into the darkroom.

Dante had clipped large photos to rope strung along the wall, photos that held images of me in Amanda's samples, photos that captured the interior of Amanda's studio. More than one captured the unflattering view of the unzipped back of the too-small red gown. If Dante hadn't been the one who took the pictures, I might have tried arguing that it wasn't me. But now two people knew about the bow on the back of my panties.

He slipped his arms around me, and I leaned back against his chest. "It's getting late. I've developed most of the photos. I can come back tomorrow to finish the rest. Unless you want me to stay..." His hands glided upward, and his lips brushed against the side of my hair.

I turned around and boosted myself up onto one of the unused counters, legs dangling down the cabinet like Joseph's legs had dangled from the folding chair out front. The red glow from the bulbs and the intimate setting of the darkroom were navigating our conversation in a direction that made me nervous. Not bad-nervous. Ramped-up-pulse nervous.

Dante's heat was palpable. His eyes were dark and mysterious. His black rockabilly pompadour gleamed with the red lights reflecting off it, and his lips were fuller than I'd noticed until now. And they were about two inches from my own.

I remembered how it had felt to kiss him last night. Soft. Tender. He placed a hand on the counter on either side of my hips and leaned in so far that his lips almost touched mine. I leaned forward and nipped at his lower lip. His fingers reached under my sweater.

A knock on the door of the garage interrupted us.

I pulled back. "That must be the detective," I said in a raspy voice. "I asked him to come over tonight."

Dante hung his head down, his hands still planted on either side of me. "Great," he said in a voice that matched my own. "We can show him the photos."

I hopped down from the counter and left. Dante followed. But when I got to the garage door and looked out the window, I knew it wasn't great at all.

Detective Loncar wasn't alone. The person with him was Amanda.

23

IT'S COLD OUT THERE

"What's Amanda Ries doing here? With my detective?" I asked out loud. To myself I added *while Dante and I were about to cross a line I wasn't sure I was ready to cross?* while also taking note of the possessive pronoun I'd applied to Loncar.

"Only one way to find out," Dante said.

I opened the door to the garage and motioned them in. Loncar's breath came out in puffs thanks to the drop in temperature. The air felt moist and cold. Like snow was on its way.

"Ms. Ries came to the police station to talk to me. I think you should hear what she has to say." He looked over my shoulder at Dante. I turned and looked at Dante too.

"I was just leaving," he said. The four of us walked through the garage and into the house. Loncar and Amanda waited in the kitchen. Dante shrugged into his motorcycle jacket and zipped it up. I walked him to the door.

"You don't have to leave," I said.

"I think I do. You went stiffer than a surfboard the

second you saw Amanda, and I'd place money on what you were thinking. I don't think it had much to do with the arson investigation. You're not over the shoe guy yet."

I blushed and turned away. The coat closet was opposite the front door, and I reached inside and pulled out a black plaid wool scarf. I draped it around Dante's neck and kept my hands on the ends. "It's cold out there."

"I'm not all that worried about the weather. Good night, Samantha."

He left. I stood by the door and watched him straddle his motorcycle, pull on his helmet, and back the bike off its kickstand. When he was out of my driveway, he cranked the engine and took off.

Breakup Rule #7: Recognize when you're not ready to move on. Amanda knew Dante was working with me in the capacity of photographer. She'd fired Clive and brought him on based on my recommendation. Catching him here at my house must have triggered questions about my real relationship with him. And while I doubted she and Detective Loncar had gotten into a discussion of my love life, Loncar had seen Dante and me together at Warehouse Five. Finding him here, after dark, might compromise my story about Dante being the official new photographer for Amanda's collection.

I joined Loncar and Amanda in the kitchen. "Can I get either of you anything?" I asked, hoping the answer was wine, pretzels, or ice cream, assuming Dante and the boys hadn't finished off two out of those three.

"No thanks," Amanda said. Loncar just shook his head.

We moved to the living room. Amanda sat in one of the arm chairs, her back to the window. Loncar kept his hand on the back of the other chair but did not sit. I, being of the why-stand-when-you-can-sit philosophy, took the sofa.

"Did something happen?" I asked.

Loncar looked at Amanda. Amanda looked at the floor.

"Ms. Ries, I assume you came here to tell Ms. Kidd what you told me earlier. Why don't you go first?"

Amanda stared at her hands like she'd just discovered they were there. She wore a set of gold rings on her left hand, and with her right she slid them up to her knuckle and back into place.

Whatever it was Loncar wanted her to tell me, she wasn't eager to share. I stared at the top of her head while she played with her jewelry. The clinking of the gold rings against each other was the only sound in the house. She looked up at me, her face pale and gaunt. "Can I use your restroom?"

"Sure. It's the room directly at the top of the stairs," I said.

She moved quickly. Soon after the door shut, I heard her retching.

"Detective, what's going on? Why did you bring Amanda with you?"

"I didn't. She must have come here after she came to me. We met up in front of your house."

"What's going on?"

Logan stuck his head out from under the sofa. The detective held his hand down, and Logan sniffed it. "Ms. Kidd, I came here to talk to you about the fire in the dumpster outside of Warehouse Five."

"Did you check it out? Did you find anything?"

"Gigger had the contents of the dumpster bagged.

They're at his office. You want to tell me what I'm looking for?"

I picked up a piece of paper and made a quick sketch of the steel disc that I'd seen by the arm hole of Eddie's mannequin "About three inches in diameter, with a hole in the middle. There are openings like triangles. It'll look like the bomb-shelter-fallout signs from the fifties."

Loncar stood up and turned his back to me. He wandered into the kitchen and made a call. When he came back, he was looking at the face of his phone, swiping through photos.

"Is this what you're talking about?" He handed me his phone.

The image on the screen matched the steel disc on the inside of the plaster mannequin joint I'd seen at Tradava.

"Yes," I said. "It's a piece of metal from a plaster mannequin. It fits around the arm holes and leg holes, so you can snap the limbs into place. That disc says that somebody burned a mannequin. But why? Why throw it out in the first place?"

"You were pretty sure you saw a leg."

"Don't you see? I did see a leg. It wasn't a person's leg. It was a mannequin leg. That's why you didn't find evidence of a person inside the dumpster."

He stared at the picture on his phone and nodded. I studied his face, looking for signs of exasperation or disbelief. There was no eye rolling. No shaking head. No rescinding his offer to listen to my theories.

I continued. "Amanda's show was at Warehouse Five, and she had mannequins in the lobby before the show."

"The mannequins at the mall are plastic. We would have smelled the burning plastic when the dumpster went up in flames. You were close to the fire. You probably would have had some fluorocarbon poisoning."

"New mannequins are plastic, but not these. They're made of plaster and metal. They're a lot heavier than the new ones. More durable too. Someone would have to be pretty strong to get one into the dumpster."

"How do you know so much about mannequins?"

"My friend Eddie Adams told me. You remember him, right? Tradava's visual director who worked the hat exhibit at the museum?"

Loncar nodded.

"When these mannequins get broken, Tradava calls a special company to dispose of them. They incinerate the mannequin and recycle the steel rods inside the torso and limbs."

"Whoever tried to burn the mannequin must not have known about the steel frame inside."

"Or whoever tried to burn the mannequin didn't care so much about destroying it. They cared about destroying whatever it was wearing."

Loncar looked up. "You think this was about destroying the clothes?"

"The rest of the clothes from Amanda's show were destroyed, weren't they?"

The water turned on upstairs, and the toilet flushed. The door opened and then shut. More throwing up.

"I think I should see if she's okay," I said.

"When I feel like that I want to be alone."

"Do you know why she feels like that?"

"I get the feeling she's not entirely happy about the reason she's here."

"Are you going to tell me what it is?"

"It's her business to tell you, not mine." He stood up. "I'm going to follow up on this mannequin lead." He waved the page with my sketches. "I'll let you know if anything comes of it."

Loncar didn't have to tell me anything if he didn't want to, and we both knew it. "I appreciate it," I said.

He nodded once and let himself out.

I went to the kitchen and filled a glass with ice and ginger ale. After climbing the stairs, I tapped gently on the bathroom door.

"Amanda, it's Samantha. The detective left." I waited a beat. She didn't respond. "I brought you ginger ale."

"Come in," she said.

Of all the places I could have imagined spending time with Amanda, my bathroom wasn't one of them. She sat on the fluffy pink carpet square by the base of the toilet with her back leaning against the wall. Her glossy black hair had been pulled back and tucked into the collar of her sweater. Her eyes were bloodshot and framed in circles that had gotten darker since she'd arrived. I held out the glass. She waved it off. She stood up and rinsed her mouth with tap water, dried her face on a hand towel, and sat back down.

"You must love this," she said. "Homicide detectives showing up at your door and me throwing up in your bathroom. Can I ask you a question?"

"Shoot."

"Why did you keep showing up to help me?"

"Because after a year of trying to do things I wasn't so good at, I wanted to do something I was."

She picked at the pink carpet fibers. "I thought I was good at designing clothes. If I'd thought for a second my career would go this way, I never would have bothered."

"Amanda, you're a fashion designer. It's a stressful job. Not arsonists-and-attackers stressful, but it's not like you spend your day in a glass cage with kittens. No matter what happens, you have to find a way to deal with the stress."

I lowered myself until I was sitting across from her. She took a sip of the ginger ale. "Is this how you felt when you first moved here? Like the walls were closing in around you and there was no way out?"

"A little."

"I didn't make things any better for you. I thought you were trouble. When Nick suggested I have you work on the show, I was afraid of what would happen."

"Are you accusing me of something?"

"No. But I was afraid that your presence would make things more difficult. My best friend's ex-girlfriend. Not exactly the qualifications I would have written up on the want ad."

"You wanted my help. And after the fire, when I came to your studio, you confided in me about those letters."

"That's what I'm trying to tell you, Samantha. That wasn't real. Everything Nick had told me about you said you weren't going to walk away when you were attacked. I couldn't deal with that, too, so I sent you on the trail of an imaginary bad guy." Her face went even more ashen. "Don't you see? There's no anonymous threat."

"But your show went up in flames, and the threats in those letters—"

"Samantha, please, listen to me. I made those letters myself."

24

THREE INGREDIENTS

I HEARD WHAT SHE SAID, BUT I DIDN'T BELIEVE HER. WE stared at each other for a few seconds before she spoke.

"I made all six of them. I cut the letters out of fashion magazines and glued them to a piece of paper and ran off a copy and showed them to you."

"But you said you gave them to the police—"

"I said if someone sent me threatening letters I would take them to the police. You misinterpreted that. All I wanted to do was to distract you from the fact that you were attacked outside of my show. I felt guilty. Especially since I'd basically just fired you. When the fire happened, he said you'd try to figure out who did it, so I made up the letters as a distraction. I would have told you about them sooner. I was going to tell you about them the day you came over for the interview, but you brought the photographer. And then I found out you told the police about them. Why? Normal people go to the police. You don't. I know you don't, because Nick told me you don't."

A part of me wondered what else Nick had told her about me.

"Then nobody's been threatening your business?"

"No." Her eyes filled with tears, and she buried her face in her hands.

Amanda was in a dark place. She was on the brink of losing everything: her business, her credibility, her future. She'd spent half an hour throwing up in my bathroom and, even though I'd been too polite to comment on it, there was a clump of vomit in her hair.

She was teetering on the edge of rock bottom.

Tentatively, I put my hand on her arm to console her. She tried to stifle her sobs, but the tears weren't going to stop anytime soon. I reached for a box of tissues and handed them to her and then sat and waited while she pulled herself together. Of all the questions that I could have asked, I avoided the biggest one of all: if Nick was her best friend, why wasn't he helping her through this crisis?

She blew her nose for the seventeenth time and set the tissue in a neat pile with the others. Her nose was red and swollen, and her eyes were puffy.

"Amanda, there's a very good chance the person who put me in the hospital was the same person who started the fire that destroyed your show. I need you to be honest with me and tell me what you told the arson investigator."

"The tall man with the short pants?" she said. For the first time since we'd met, we shared a smile. "I gave him a statement, but I didn't have much to say. The fire started on the runway. I was backstage, making sure the models were perfect before they went out. You probably saw more than I did."

"I have the show on videotape. Do you want to see what you missed?"

In a move of extreme compassion, I offered Amanda the use of my shower before we watched the video. I was still reeling from her confession. The self-proclaimed normal woman with the model appearance and the glamorous business had gone a little crazy. I guess we all go a little crazy sometimes.

While she was showering, I went downstairs. There was still the matter of food—or lack of food—to be dealt with, and even though Amanda and I were forging new ground in how we related to each other, I wasn't yet ready to let her see my shortcomings. There was only one person I could call.

"Yo," I said when Eddie answered. "I'm in over my head, and I need your help."

"Are you okay? Where are you?"

"I'm at home, but I'm not alone."

"Which one? Nick or Dante?"

"Neither." I held my breath and glanced up the stairs. "Amanda."

"Is Mercury in retrograde?"

"We don't have enough time for the full explanation. Here's the problem. She's in a bad way, and I don't think she should be alone. But I haven't eaten since nine o'clock this morning, and that was a bowl of ice cream. And I know this is petty of me, but I feel like I have a chance to prove something about myself to her, and I don't want to order delivery."

"I'm pulling an all-nighter on these displays. I can't bring you food. Tell me what we have to work with."

"I have two partially defrosted chicken breasts, a bag of

baby carrots, less than a third of a half gallon of Neapolitan ice cream, three bags of pretzels, and a box of wine."

"How close have you guys gotten since she's been there?"

"Uncharted territory."

"Okay, so save the pretzels and the wine and get out a large stockpot. I'm going to tell you how to make chicken soup."

"Sounds complicated."

"How complicated can it be? You have three ingredients."

"Good point." I got out the stockpot and came back to the phone.

"Bring four cups of water to a boil. Hopefully your chicken will be defrosted by this point. Add the chicken and chopped-up carrots. Throw in some salt and pepper, cover, and let it simmer for half an hour."

"And then what?"

"And then you pour it into a bowl and eat it."

"That's it?"

"Dude, we are going to work on this. Now, is everything else okay?"

"Not even close."

After hanging up, I put the water on to boil and submerged the package of chicken breasts in warm water to get them fully defrosted. My mind wandered to Amanda's motivation while I chopped the baby carrots. When the water in the stock pot was boiling, I added the chicken breasts and the carrots, shook in some salt and pepper, and closed the lid again. I set the microwave timer for thirty minutes and poured myself a generous glass of wine. I'd earned it.

Ten minutes later, Amanda came downstairs and joined me in the living room. "Something smells good," she said.

"I'm making chicken soup. I thought it might make you feel better." I didn't mention that it was either that or pretzels, and that I didn't consider her worthy of my pretzel stash.

"I thought you didn't cook?" she asked.

"I can cook when I have to," I said defensively. The timer beeped, and I stood. "Have a seat. We can eat out here and watch the video. I'll be right back."

We traded spaces, and I went into the kitchen, returning with a wooden tray that held two bowls of soup. "I don't have any crackers," I said.

"This is already more than I expected. Thank you."

Amanda swept her hair back over her left shoulder. She wasn't one to overdo her makeup routine, but without any, she was still a knockout. She balanced her bowl on her lap and scooped dainty mouthfuls of broth to her lips. If she hadn't been sitting in my living room, I would have held the bowl up to my lips and drank. Heck, if she hadn't been there, I would have bribed Eddie to show up with hoagies.

I hit play on the remote, and the screen filled with the image from the stationary camera at the end of Amanda's runway. She looked up and froze for a moment, her spoon halfway to her mouth. The broth dribbled from the spoon and spilled onto her camel trousers. She glanced down at the spreading wet spot but didn't dab it.

This was the fifth time I'd watch it, and I hoped to see something I'd missed the first four. There were Dante and I on the left. There was Clive on the right. At the twenty-seven second mark, there was Santangelo sneaking in. I glanced at Amanda to see if she'd noticed, but she did not.

The lights went down, the pop music started, and the runway came alive. Godzilla graphics illuminated the back wall above Amanda's name. And then five models came down the runway before Harper in the silver wig and kimono.

"She complained that her kimono didn't fit. Remember?" I said. "But aside from how the sleeves are dragging on the floor, it looks great on her."

Amanda leaned forward. "It's going to happen now, isn't it?" she asked quietly.

I nodded.

I knew where to look for the smoke. It appeared on the left first, by the hem of the kimono, a whisper of something, and then flames. It was that fast. Screams replaced music. The house lights went on. Harper struggled to take off the kimono. Nick stepped out from behind the backdrop and helped her. The fire blazed a trail through the rose petals on the ground and spread to the rest of the room. Someone knocked the camera over, and the video went to static.

"So that's what happened," Amanda said when it was done. "We couldn't see anything. We didn't know. One second I was adjusting a collar on one of the girls, and the next, Harper was screaming."

"How did Nick know Harper needed his help? If you were all so busy backstage, how come he knew to come out and help her out of the kimono?"

"There was a small video feed on a monitor in the back. Tiny watched the monitor to keep up with the pace and make sure there weren't any problems out front. Nick must have been watching too."

"Where was Clive Barrington through all of this?"

"I don't know, and I know how that sounds, but you

know what it's like backstage at a runway show. It's chaos! I love the excitement, but I had to concentrate on the problem in front of me. Otherwise I get overwhelmed by how little I can control. That's why I have Tiny watching the monitor and the interns to help dress the models and Nick to oversee the accessories. There's almost too much to do, but it would be worse to have people helping who I can't trust."

"That's why you let me go on Friday night, isn't it?" I asked. She looked up at me, and we locked eyes. "You didn't know if you could trust me. You knew how stressful it would be, and you knew I knew the collection. There was no good reason for you to let me go before the show. And if you hadn't fired me, I wouldn't have left when I did, and I might not have been attacked."

"I've been over that decision a hundred times since then. Honestly, Samantha, I didn't want to let you go."

"Then why did you?"

"Because I couldn't stand what it was doing to Nick. I'm not sure how much more he can handle."

"What does Nick have to do with you letting me go?"

She pushed her soup bowl away and sat back. "You don't know, do you?"

"Know what?"

"Nick's father is in the hospital."

25

REALITY BITES

My heart stopped. Tears built up a wall behind my eyes. I set the soup bowl down. "When?"

"A few weeks ago. He's been splitting his time between Ribbon and New York."

"What happened?"

"His dad fell and broke his hip."

"Is he going to be okay?"

"It's still too soon to tell."

"Why didn't Nick say anything?"

"What did you want him to say? You broke his heart, and you moved on like nothing happened."

"That's what you think? Is that what Nick thinks?"

"What do you want us to think? You brought a date to my runway show. You told Nick you needed a change. And the guy you're dating is my new photographer."

"He used to work for a private investigator. He's a good person to have on the inside."

"Depends on what you're trying to accomplish."

I looked at my soup bowl for a few seconds. "Me

working with you after Nick fired me—that wasn't his idea, was it? It was yours."

She shrugged. "You two were making each other crazy. At least that's how it sounded to me."

"He talked to you about me?"

"Don't you talk to Eddie about Nick?"

"That's different."

"How?"

How to tell her that I had an irrational jealousy of her because I didn't know the details of her past with Nick? That even though I'd known him for nine years, I secretly hated that she'd known him longer? That some might say people who ate ice cream for breakfast weren't in the same league as she was? I went with "Maybe it isn't different. It just feels like it is."

"He wanted to make sure you were going to be okay."

"Does he know about the letters?"

"No. That was—that was my own idea. He's dealing with a lot right now, and I thought if I could keep you preoccupied, you'd be one less thing for him to worry about."

"How is his dad?"

She shrugged. "I don't know. We haven't talked much over this past week. He has his problems, and I have mine." She tucked her feet under her and picked at the carpet fibers. "I went to design school so I could get into fashion. One thing led to another, and now here I am. I guess you never know when the bottom's going to drop out of your life."

"Amanda, you have a gift. Don't let any of this stop you from using it. This," I gestured toward the screen, "is all a set-back, sure, but don't let it get in the way of what you want out of life."

The longer Amanda sat on my sofa, the less jealousy I felt toward her. She'd relied on the people around her to see her vision through, and she found herself alone. Did she have a chance at success if she was willing to hand control of her business over to others? Was it possible for her to succeed if she didn't?

Amanda yawned, and then so did I. I'd lost all track of time, but I suspected it was late. Hours had passed since Loncar and Amanda showed up and Dante had left, and for a moment I wished I could pretend that none of this had happened. But I couldn't. Because all of it had. The breakup. The attack. The fire. And now, Nick's dad. Things had gotten very, very real.

Something had happened since the breakup. Somewhere between learning that Dante had a son, Detective Loncar had a wife who made uncooked meatloaf, and Amanda had a nervous stomach, I realized that I'd kept myself from seeing reality when it came to Nick. I'd projected my feelings onto him, the daydreams that I'd had when he was a shoe designer and I was a buyer, when we couldn't do much more than casually flirt over chocolate soufflés at Market Week.

And once we'd started dating, I wanted him to see me as perfect girlfriend material. The reality? He was coping with the very real crisis of his father's declining health, while I was with his maybe-former girlfriend eating three-ingredient chicken soup.

Reality bites.

I carried the empty bowls to the kitchen so Amanda wouldn't see the sadness on my face. The clock read eleven thirty. Dante's developed photos awaited me in the darkroom, but they felt less important now that I knew the threats against Amanda had been fake.

I was working up the best way to politely suggest that playtime was over when I returned to the living room and found her asleep on the sofa. I pulled a spare comforter out of the closet and covered her. I pointed a finger at the ceiling. "I get extra credit for this, you got that?"

It was well past my bedtime, and my body was tired and achy. I climbed into bed. I dreamt about fires and woke up in a sweat with the covers kicked onto the floor. I'd been so buried in details about Amanda's samples that I hadn't stopped to ask the most obvious question of all: How had someone started the fire in the middle of a runway show in the first place?

26

GOLD STAR FOR PERSONAL GROWTH

THE NEXT MORNING, I WOKE UP ALONE IN THE HOUSE. Amanda had left a note on the coffee table thanking me for my generosity. That was it. No acknowledgment of the fake letters. No apology for firing me on the eve of her runway show. No mention of the homemade chicken soup. I peeked out the front window to confirm her departure. Her car was gone.

I showered and dressed in a man's white button-down oxford under a chunky gray knit sweater with a Union Jack on the front, a short, pleated gray-and-navy plaid skirt, tights layered with argyle knee socks, and black leather riding boots. I slipped on black fingerless gloves for the simple reason that they made me feel tough.

I opened and shut the freezer and refrigerator. Now that I'd cooked the chicken breasts and the carrots, the only thing left was a carton of Cool Whip left over from a Labor Day party. Surprisingly, it looked exactly as it had months ago. I dragged my index finger though the white fluffy substance and tasted it. Seemed fresh enough. But then I thought of last night. I'd made chicken soup from scratch. In personal growth terms, wouldn't it be taking a step backward to have Cool Whip for breakfast?

I called Eddie. "How'd things go at Tradava last night?"

"I wrapped up around two thirty."

"I thought when you got promoted to visual director, you'd be able to delegate a little?"

"Dude, I'm not management material. I got into creative work so I could be creative. Telling other people what to do isn't my style."

"Funny, I don't remember you having a problem with it when I helped you out at the museum," I said. "Where are you?" I asked.

"Home. Why?"

"Can you pick up breakfast and come over here? I need to talk out a few things."

"Do these things include your slumber party with Amanda?"

"Yes."

"I'll be there in twenty."

To hear Eddie say it, you could get from any point of Ribbon to any other point in precisely twenty minutes. The estimation was surprisingly accurate. The doorbell rang about twenty minutes later. I checked the peephole. Eddie was on the porch, holding a brown paper bag.

He handed it to me, and I pulled out two breakfast sandwiches wrapped in wax paper. They appeared to be the same, so I handed him one.

He looked at the wrapper and swapped them out. "Trust me," he said.

I poured two mugs full of coffee and joined him at the dining-room table.

"You are not going to believe what Amanda told me last night. Get this: after the fire, she showed me these threatening letters against her company. She made them up to send me off on the trail of a criminal who didn't exist."

"Which you're doing, so it worked."

"It started out with me wanting to know who jumped me. That turned into wanting to know who set the fire at the show, because I think the two things are related. But then there was a fire in the dumpster outside of Warehouse Five the day after the show. I can't figure that out. Was someone trying to destroy evidence? Or did they know I was there and wanted to scare me?"

"Dude, you've been busy. Back up. What's this about another fire?"

"After you left me at Brothers, Dante and I went to Warehouse Five. It was his idea," I added before he could make any more comments about me doing exactly what Amanda suspected. "He thought we might notice something."

"Did you?"

"That's the thing. He was on one side of the building taking pictures. I went to the other side because that's where I was attacked. My car had been sitting in the lot the whole time. I moved the flyers from the windshield to the front passenger side and sat inside. Something moved near the dumpster. I drove closer to check it out and smelled smoke. Right after I saw a leg sticking out, the dumpster caught on fire."

"A leg?" he said.

"A mannequin leg."

"That's why you got all juiced up when I told you about the mannequins."

"I told Loncar about it. At first, I thought it was a body or an amputated limb. He said they didn't find any evidence of a body inside, and the fire hadn't been burning long enough to completely destroy a corpse."

Eddie set down his sandwich and his face turned a greenish shade. He pulled a pill vial out of his pocket and swallowed a white tablet. "Dramamine. It'll help with the nausea."

"Are you getting sick?"

"I'm trying to eat while you're talking about disembodied limbs burning up in dumpsters. A little nausea is normal."

Eddie was right. I hadn't even flinched at Amanda being sick last night, and now my best friend was popping anti-nausea pills like Skittles. Were dismembered limbs and dead bodies becoming yet another thing that I compartmentalized?

"We don't have to talk about this," I said. "Let's talk about something else. What's going on with you?"

"Me? The usual. Working round the clock to get the store ready. Nab four or five hours of sleep and then do it all over again."

"All work and no play makes Eddie a dull boy," I said.

"I've got a two-week vacation coming up. Going to Miami Beach. I'll make up for lost time as soon as that plane lands."

"You're okay with that? Work like a crazy person, go away to recharge, and come back and do it all over again?"

"That's how life works. At least since you moved here, there's a new element to the mix."

"Yep, that's me. All fun and games until somebody gets

hurt." I swallowed a disturbing amount of coffee and coughed.

"The Dramamine has taken effect. Hit me with whatever you have."

I leaned forward and tapped my index finger on the table. "Here's what I want to know. Why would someone want to attack me? Was I the target all along? I don't think so. The fact that there have been no other physical attacks makes me think my attack was a message to Amanda. One of her staffers gets hospitalized. Warning!" I made jazz hands on either side of my head. "Somebody wants you to fail!"

"It *is* starting to look like somebody's had it in for Amanda all along."

"That's what I thought, but mostly because of the threats she made up. Now I need to come up with a different angle." I ticked off what I knew on my fingers. "First I was attacked, and there was a fire. Then the second fire during her show. Third in the parking lot outside of the venue where she held her show. The fire on the runway would have been enough to ruin her. I don't know why someone set the third fire."

"Do you have to? I mean, this is Amanda Ries we're talking about. She fired you. She faked evidence to send you chasing after phantoms. And she's Nick's ex-girlfriend."

"We don't know that last part. We only suspect it."

"Dude, this isn't the time to play dumb," he said.

"Fine. She's Nick's ex-girlfriend. But the woman spent an hour throwing up in my bathroom last night. Did I sneak in and take blackmail photos? No. I made her chicken soup."

"Great. You get a gold star for personal growth. That doesn't mean you have to solve her problems for her."

"I know I don't owe her anything. I know I should just

walk away. And I know the fact that I don't proves everything everybody says about me is right."

We stared at each other for a few seconds, an entire conversation of acceptance and understanding taking place between a raised eyebrow, a smile, and a shrug. Then Eddie turned his head to the side. "Do you smell burnt toast?"

I sniffed the air. "Yes."

"Okay, good. I thought it was my imagination." He picked up his breakfast sandwich and took another bite.

"Why do we both smell burnt toast? We're not making breakfast."

We turned our heads toward the front of the house. Through the picture window I saw orange flames shooting out from an open trash can sitting in the middle of my driveway.

27

STOP WASTING MY TIME

"Fire!" I yelled. I ran out the front door. Eddie followed.

The trash can sat behind Eddie's VW Bug. I crept closer to see what was burning inside, but the heat from the flames kept me back.

"Call someone," I said. I raced back inside for the fire extinguisher that was under the kitchen sink and returned. My cold fingers fumbled with the pin. I pulled it loose. I aimed the nozzle at the fire and squeezed the handle. A blast of compressed carbon dioxide shot out like a cloud of snow. The pressure caught me by surprise, and I was knocked off balance. I scrambled to my feet and started again. The spray covered the inside of the metal can until the flames were extinguished. I stepped back and dropped the canister. Across the street, Mrs. Iova's curtains opened, and she looked out. I was shaking too badly to make a face or a rude gesture like the other neighbors did when they caught her spying.

Minutes later, I heard a siren growing close. A red fire

truck turned at the corner and raced toward my house. Several men jumped down and uncoiled the hose, ready to act.

"Where's the fire?" one asked.

"It was in there." I pointed at the trash can.

He crept forward and looked inside the receptacle. "How'd it start?"

"I don't know."

"Where were you?"

"Inside my house."

"You throw away anything flammable?"

"I didn't throw away anything at all. This isn't my trash can." He looked at me like I was a nuisance. "Can you call Inspector Gigger or Detective Loncar at the Ribbon Police?"

"You know them?"

"Yes. I'm helping"—no, that wouldn't go over all that well— "I've been a witness at other fires in Ribbon. I think I should talk to them."

He stood a few feet away from me, suited up in his fireman garb. His fellow firefighters scattered around the end of my driveway, their testosterone and adrenaline levels in need of a release. I felt like I was throwing a party for twenty and only had one cupcake to serve for dessert.

Eddie stood on the front porch with Logan over one shoulder. Eddie's eyes were wide. He set Logan inside the house and pulled the front door shut. He sat on the front porch step, and I joined him. The sudden fear of fire had kept me from noticing the chill in the air, but now that I stopped and sat, I felt the cold through to my bones. I went inside and pulled two wool blankets from the hall closet and returned outside, handing one to Eddie.

Inspector Gigger's shiny silver car pulled up behind the

fire truck. He approached the group of men and exchanged words with the chief and then strode across the lot to us. Pieces of ash flitted through the air like gray snow flurries. I stood up and wrapped the blanket around me tighter.

"Ms. Kidd," he said. "What can you tell me about this fire?"

"My friend Eddie and I were inside the house. We smelled something burning. As soon as we saw the flames in the trash can, I came back in for my fire extinguisher, and Eddie called the fire department."

"How do you think this fire got started?"

"I don't know."

"What was in the trash can?"

"I don't know. It's not my trash can."

"Where did it come from?"

This was getting tiring. "I don't know."

"Ms. Kidd, it's a stretch to think you didn't have anything to do with this, so stop wasting my time. I want to know how you started the fire. Timing device? Remote detonator? Or perhaps your friend did it for you?"

"That doesn't even make sense! We were inside. Ask my neighbors. Somebody must have seen us run outside and put out the fire. Ask Mrs. Iova over there. She spies on everybody. She must have seen something."

"I find it hard to believe your trash can spontaneously combusted."

I jumped up, and the blanket fell from my shoulders. "Inspector Gigger," I said, taking a step toward him, "I don't know what you've heard about me, but I am not in the habit of setting fires to get attention."

"But you do like the attention you get from playing amateur sleuth, don't you?" He reached inside his coat and pulled out a newspaper clipping. Deliberately, he unfolded it and held it so it was facing me. It was the article that had run about me after my involvement in the recent museum murder.

"That is a human-interest story that grew out of the fact that I did something good."

"That is true." He glanced at the newspaper. "Nice photo, by the way." He folded the newspaper clipping up and put it back into his pocket. "But arson is a crime of attention seeking. Three fires, Ms. Kidd. Three fires where you've been present. Four if we count your so-called attack. It raises questions."

"It wasn't so-called, it was! And what about the mannequin leg in the dumpster at the warehouse? I know you must know by now that it was a mannequin leg. I called Detective Loncar as soon as I figured that out. He confirmed that I was right."

"Ms. Kidd, you're friends with the visual director of a store that uses mannequins. There's another way that you could have been right about that without using your considerable powers of deduction."

It was worse to hear him insinuate that Eddie was involved too. "I don't need to listen to this," I said. "Someone set a fire in my driveway, and I called 911. If I'd done anything other than that, people would have wondered why. But I do exactly what I'm supposed to do, and I get accused of rigging fires all over town?"

Loncar's unwashed car pulled up behind Gigger's silver one. As soon as the detective was out of the car, he scanned the scene. I pointed at him. "From now on, I will only talk to him." I stormed past Eddie and into the house. I didn't bother slamming the door. Whoever wanted to follow me could.

A few minutes later, the detective came inside with the head fireman. He closed the door, and Logan came out from under the sofa and ran his head against the detective's trouser leg. Loncar picked him up, scratched his ears, and set him back down. Logan took off up the carpeted stairs to the bedrooms.

The head fireman stayed by Loncar's side. He looked to be about fifty-something, with deep creases by his eyes and mouth. His hair was mostly gray, matted to his head from the fire helmet he now held in his hand.

"Where's Eddie?" I asked.

"He's giving his statement to Gigger," Loncar said. "Why don't you get me caught up?"

"Eddie and I were in the kitchen talking about Amanda." I met Loncar's stare. "Oh, come on. She's my ex-boyfriend's maybe-former girlfriend. If I didn't talk about her behind her back, people would think there was something wrong with me."

"Go on."

"We smelled something burning. Eddie described it as burnt toast. I was facing the windows and saw the flames out of the top of the trash can. I tried to get close to see what was inside, but it was too hot. I got my fire extinguisher from the kitchen, and Eddie called 911. Gigger can probably tell you the rest."

"You did a good job putting out the flames," the fireman said.

"It's not my first time with a fire extinguisher," I said, thinking back to an unsuccessful attempt at deep frying. "Do you know what was burning?"

The fireman shook his head. "There's nothing left. Whatever was on fire is now a pile of ash. You say your friend smelled burnt toast?"

"That's what he said. I smelled something burning, but I didn't connect it with anything in particular except maybe the time I scorched my pajamas with a flat iron."

The fireman's eyes moved to my newly bobbed hair. "You gave up the flat iron?"

"Temporarily." I settled in on the sofa. "We might have assumed that someone burned their breakfast if we hadn't seen the flames. They were big, like three feet higher than the top of the trash can. I wouldn't swear by it, but the flames seemed smaller by the time I came back and put it out. Like it would have put itself out without my help."

"You might be right. The aluminum trash can contained the fire pretty well. Since there's nothing left inside to tell us what was burning, it could be that the ignited object burned away completely. No scent of chemicals means it was organic."

"You're not going to say it was an accident, are you?"

"No. But if the arsonist rigged things to burn themselves out, he probably didn't want to stick around to see how it unfolded. Makes me think it was a message."

"Your men seemed a little annoyed when they got here."

"Not annoyed. There's a certain adrenaline rush that helps them act fast and minimize the threat of an open fire. When they arrived and the fire was out, they were left with all this adrenaline and nothing to act on."

Loncar's turn to ask questions. "You put out the fire, the firemen arrived, and then what?"

"Then nothing. Gigger arrived and accused me of being

the common thread at all the fires. You showed up somewhere around there."

"He's right, you know. You were present each time." He held up his hand palm-side out. "I'm not saying you set the fires. I'm not saying it's anything more than coincidence. But you best think about that, because there's a chance you can offer us a lead we don't have."

I leaned forward and held my head in my hands. The room went silent while they waited for me to come up with a theory. "I don't know what lead you think I can come up with. This fire was in front of a private residence. It was a message because it's *my* private residence, but that doesn't mean it makes any more sense."

"Ms. Kidd, if there's anything you remember from any of the other fires, I'd like to hear it. I think the fire captain would like to hear it too."

I looked back and forth between Loncar and the captain's faces. They weren't treating me like I was a nuisance. Instead of ridiculous accusations like Gigger's, Loncar had asked me for help. Politely too!

Before I could say anything, a fireman burst through the front door. His helmet was back in place, and his chest was puffed out like a cage fighter at go time.

"Yo, Cap, we gotta leave. There's been another fire downtown." He rattled off an address. The captain jumped up and ran out of my house.

And I sat on the sofa, feeling like someone had dumped a ten-pound bag of ice down the back of my shirt.

The new fire was at Amanda's studio.

28

NONE OF IT HELPED

WITHIN SECONDS THE FIREMEN WERE GONE. GIGGER PUT A Kojak light on top of his car and sped away from the curb. Eddie stood with Loncar and me on the front step.

"Aren't you going with them?" I asked Loncar.

"No. I'm going to stay here and find out what caused that light bulb to go off over your head when you heard the address of the fire."

The detective was getting very good at reading my expressions.

I turned and went into the living room. Loncar and Eddie followed. Eddie and I shared the sofa, and Loncar sat in one of the arm chairs.

"What's your theory, Ms. Kidd?"

"That's Amanda Ries's studio," I said. "You wanted a theory? What about this: Amanda spent the night here after you left." I sat up, and my eyes darted around at various items in the living room while I thought. "I don't know when she left. I woke up, and there was a note on the table. Either I was sound asleep, or she was abnormally quiet. Maybe whoever set this fire thinks she lives here. Which would make Amanda the common thread, if you consider that there have now been fires at her show, in the parking lot outside of where her show was, here, and now at her studio."

"Any thoughts on why someone would be out to get Ms. Ries?"

"None. She's the most law-abiding citizen I could imagine." Eddie nodded his head in agreement. "But it seems like somebody is keeping tabs on her whereabouts. Did you ever follow up with Santangelo Toma? About the ID that you found by the dumpster outside of the warehouse? Or the fire? Either fire?"

"Yes."

"And?" A new thought hit me. "His name is San-TANGELO. Tangelos are a close cousin of oranges. Like what were used to beat me up. Are you following me?"

Eddie's eyes went wide. "Dude, that's creepy."

"I know. It's like a calling card or something."

Loncar crossed his arms over his coat and cleared his throat. We turned our attention to him.

"We confirmed with Ms. Ries that the fruit she found around you was part of the food service for the staff and models."

"Santangelo has a studio at Warehouse Five. He could have swiped the fruit and jumped me. It could have been him."

"Mr. Toma is not your man." Loncar stood up. "Thank you for your cooperation, Ms. Kidd. Be careful."

I stood up too. "Detective, I'm curious. If I graduated from your citizen's police academy, would you take me more seriously?"

"Trust me, I take you very seriously." He buttoned two buttons on his wrinkled coat and left. Eddie followed him out the door and drove off behind him.

I wandered around the living room, straightening magazines on the table, moving coffee cups into the kitchen. At one point I loaded and started the dishwasher, and then I vacuumed.

None of it helped.

I pulled a navy blue pea coat over my sweater and skirt and went outside. The aluminum trash can was out of the way. I crossed the driveway and looked inside. The only thing left from the fire was a small residue of ash in the bottom center. I went back inside and found a mostly-empty eye-shadow compact in the bathroom. I tapped the remaining clump of purple powder loose and went back to the trash can to retrieve a sample of the ash. I was only able to come up with two pinches, but for my purposes, it would do. I clicked the eye-shadow case shut.

Back inside, I went to the darkroom and pulled my old chemistry set from the baker's rack. A giant spider, startled by the sudden activity, sprung to life from the pile of photos. I screamed, jumped backward, banged my hip on the corner of the counter behind me, and screamed again. I didn't know where the spider had disappeared to, so I had to be quick.

The last time I used this chemistry set was when I was ten. Although my dad had high hopes of me following in his scientific footsteps, I'd traded the lure of the beaker and microscope for the mall at an early age, and the only chemicals I was interested in were the ones that straightened my naturally curly hair. The chemistry set had been shelved and forgotten. I swatted at the box with a broom handle as a warning to any other bugs living inside, and when nothing appeared, carried the box upstairs.

On the second floor of the house, my bedroom sat to the right, the bathroom sat directly in front of me, and my sister's old room was to my left. I'd had the notion to convert it to a closet a few months ago, lining the perimeter with cheap white floor-to-ceiling bookcases that housed off-season shoes, handbags, scarves, and jewelry. A rolling rod had been pushed to the back wall. It held two dozen sleeveless dresses that wouldn't see the light of day until sometime in May.

I set the microscope on the desk and found a clean glass slide. With the tweezers that came with the set, I pinched a small amount of ash from the eye-shadow compact and placed it onto the glass. The glass went under the microscope, and I put my eye on the lens. Mixed with purple granules that could only be residue eye shadow were lots of gray stringy things and a long golden thread with a black stripe down the center.

I twisted around and scanned the clothes on the rack. A red sheath dress by the end of the rack had a torn hem. I pulled at a loose thread until it snapped off, and I set that on a new slide. The color was different, but the texture was similar to the gray stringy things. I found an empty beaker in the box and dropped the red thread in and then ran downstairs for the grill lighter that I used to ignite the wicks in burned-down candles. Back upstairs, I lit the red thread and watched it curl up and then dissolve into ash. I put the ash on the slide and looked at that.

It was pretty darn close to the gray stringy things.

So, the gray stringy things were threads. Then what was the golden rod with the black core? I had a hunch.

When Eddie had evened out my hair, he'd suggested that I donate what I chopped off to a wigmaker. It sounded like a good idea, the kind of thing I'd like to be thought of as doing. I'd put my chopped-off ponytails in a one-gallon plastic bag and left it on the sink.

The other thing I was thought of as doing was procrastinating, which was why the bag of my hair was still where I'd left it. I pulled a strand out of the bag and carried it to my desk. I knew what I wanted to see when I looked at it under the microscope.

It was the same structure as the golden thread. Which meant it wasn't a thread. It was a strand of hair. Golden hair.

A quick Google search told me that dark hair that's been chemically treated maintains its original color at the center. The golden strand with the dark core came from a not-natural blond.

Clive Barrington wasn't a natural blond. Dante had made a comment about Clive's hair color before the runway show.

I went back into the house and called my dad. We weren't the sort of family to talk every day, but I'd learned to balance my I'm-involved-in-a-murder-investigation-again calls with questions about house maintenance so he and my mom wouldn't worry too much about me. To them, I'd been frozen in time around ten years old. My older sister had been the one with babysitting jobs and child-in-charge responsibilities. I'd never been trusted with anything, not because I couldn't handle it, but because, to them, I'd always be "the kid." A shrink would probably theorize that the sense of never having grown up was why it had been so important for me to buy this particular house. I couldn't disagree, which was why I never started therapy.

"Hi Dad, it's the kid," I said.

"Hey, kid, what's up? Everything okay in the ol' PA?" he asked. He'd started speaking in rhyme since moving to California. I attributed it to the side effect of all that constant sun.

"I have a science question for you. Would a brown hair and a blond hair look the same under a microscope?"

"Nope."

"Do you mean no, or did you just say 'nope' because it rhymed with 'microscope?'"

He chuckled into the phone, and then his tone turned from Dr. Seuss to scientist. "You have to consider different factors. Is the hair color treated? If so, how long ago? Environment plays a factor, too, as does genetics. And then consider what people put on their hair: gel, mousse, hair spray—"

I wanted information, but I could already see that this could go on for a while. I cut him off. "I'm looking at a hair under a microscope. At least I think it's a hair. It's long and gold, but it has a black core."

"Where'd you get the microscope?"

"It's the one you gave me for my tenth birthday." I paused for a second, wondering if he would be impressed. My next thought was about why he'd kept it all these years. Maybe this was the very moment he'd been waiting for.

"Did you check the hair against a control group?"

"I looked at one of my own hairs under the microscope. It's the same texture, but it's dark all the way through."

"What's your conclusion?"

"I think they're both human hairs, but the gold one was dyed."

"Does that information tell you anything?"

"It sure does. Thanks for helping me, Dad, but I have to go."

"Hey, kid?" His tone shifted from scientist to dad. "How come you didn't want to play with the chemistry set when I bought it for you?"

It only took a second to answer. "Because maybe I had to grow up before I saw the value in figuring things out on my own."

29

OUR CASE

AFTER ASSURING MY DAD THAT I WASN'T IN TROUBLE, I CALLED Amanda's studio. No answer. I called her cell. No answer. I called Detective Loncar, whom I had reprogrammed from "Fuzz" to "Partner?"

"Loncar," he answered.

"Detective, hi, it's Samantha Kidd. I have more information to show you."

"I'm at the station."

"I'm on my way."

I grabbed the photos and placed the hair samples in a plastic bag in my handbag. I didn't pack my childhood microscope. There was something about the Fisher-Price logo that might have made Loncar take me less seriously.

I parked in a visitor space. Even though this wasn't the first time I'd gone to the police station to provide information, the idea of walking in still made me nervous.

Once inside, I checked in with the desk sergeant. He pressed a couple of buttons on his phone and mumbled something into the receiver. Seconds later, Loncar came to the lobby to greet me. I followed him over the freshly-mopped-yet-not-clean linoleum tile floor, through a door marked Questioning, to his office. He sat behind the worn wooden desk, and I lowered myself into the worn vinyl chair facing him. Since the last time I'd been here, a plastic bowl filled with individually wrapped sour balls sat on the corner of his desk. He caught me looking at them.

"Take one if you want. They're sugar free. My wife's on a health kick, and everything I like is off limits."

"No, thank you." I stared at the sour balls. Something about them bothered me.

He opened the bottom drawer of his desk and pulled out a bag of carrot sticks. "Sugar-free candy and carrot sticks. This is my life."

"Did you know if you chop up carrots and boil them with a chicken and salt and pepper, you get soup?" I asked.

"I thought you didn't cook," he said.

I changed the subject. "Do you think it's strange that I keep getting involved in criminal investigations around Ribbon?"

He looked surprised but not taken aback. "It's not how the rest of the residents live," he said.

"That's not what I mean. Does it indicate a personality flaw?"

"That you like to figure things out? No." He uncrossed his arms and folded his hands on top of his desk. "I have a daughter around your age. You two"—he paused—"have some things in common. Then again, in some ways you couldn't be more different." He leaned back. "Are you close to your family?"

It was a good question. Living in the house where I'd

grown up made me feel close to my family, but truth was, our lives were separate.

"We Kidds are an independent lot. We're like gypsies."

"I don't know many gypsies who move back to the town where they grew up in order to ground themselves."

Darn that Detective Loncar. He had a point. "When my parents told me they were moving to California and selling the house, I realized this was the last place I'd lived where I felt like I belonged to something. Now they're living their life, and I'm trying to live mine."

"If you got into trouble—real trouble—would you turn to them for help?"

"I like to think if I needed them, they'd be there for me."

"Five years ago, my daughter was engaged and had a good job. Now she's pregnant and alone. She won't talk about who the father is. She won't talk about why she broke things off. She's back in touch with her ex, but I'm pretty sure he's not the guy. Besides, he's moved on. She acts like my wife and I are going to punish her for making bad decisions."

"Are you?"

"She's our daughter. We want her to be happy." He stared out the window for a few seconds. "You said you figured something out. What do you have for me?"

Back to business. "That fire in the trash can in front of my house. I think it was set by Clive Barrington."

"Is that an accusation or a fact?"

"Back up for a second," I said, considering the scientific approach of my dad. I pulled the envelope of ash out from my handbag and set it on Loncar's desk. "Inside that envelope is a sample of hair that I found in the bottom of the trash bin from my driveway. I analyzed it and determined that it's been dyed blond. That is a fact. Clive Barrington has highlights, which would look the same as dark hair that's been lightened. That is also a fact. I concluded that Clive may have been the person to set the fire."

Loncar took the envelope. "That is a good piece of deduction, Ms. Kidd. There's only one problem with your theory."

"What's that?"

"Clive Barrington is in Tahiti."

"When did he leave Ribbon?"

"Yesterday. He's on a photo shoot. He checked in with us before he left because he knew he was part of an open investigation."

How very considerate of him. "What if he checked in with you to make sure you knew he had an alibi, and then he arranged for more fires while he was gone? Wouldn't that throw you off his scent?"

"Would that be the scent of burnt toast?" he asked.

"Burnt crumpets is more like it," I said, even though I don't think he expected an answer.

"Ms. Kidd, I appreciate that you brought this information to me, but answer this. How would Mr. Barrington's hair have gotten into the trash can if he wasn't at the scene?"

"Maybe it was his trash can."

Loncar leaned back. For the first time since we'd met, the buttons on his shirt did not strain over his belly.

"Let me get this straight," I said. "You're not even considering Clive as a suspect in your investigation?"

"Ms. Kidd, do I need to remind you that there has been no body? There have been no reported deaths. My only role in this is to help Inspector Gigger find an arsonist before somebody dies. We've had four fires so far, and nobody's been injured. I'd like to keep it that way."

"Nobody's been injured except *me*."

"You weren't injured in a fire."

"The attack on me is being considered separate from the arsons? Even though everything is Amanda centric?"

"Unless you can provide additional information about that attack, I'm afraid we don't have any leads to work with."

A red button lit on Loncar's phone. He held his hand in a hold-on-a-minute gesture and answered. He told the person on the other end that he was finishing up now. He hung up and caught me trying to read the incoming call number upside down.

"Ms. Kidd, this job isn't all hotlines and anonymous tips. Sometimes a phone call is just a phone call."

"So that wasn't related to our case?"

He crossed his arms again. "You got anything else for me?"

"Nope."

He stood, and I followed suit. "Thank you for your cooperation. I'll share your findings with Ichabod." He cracked a smile.

Loncar followed me out of his office. I stopped at the exit doors. "You never did tell me what you found out about Santangelo Toma," I said.

"Goodbye, Ms. Kidd."

———

I DROVE TO WAREHOUSE FIVE. Detective Loncar might have thought he was doing me a favor by ignoring my question, but as far as favors went, his was up there with gifting me brussels sprouts for my birthday.

I parked by the front lobby doors of the warehouse and went inside. If I'd expected someone to stop me, they didn't. There was nobody at the information desk, and most of the doors to the studios were shut. I wandered down the hallway and tried a few of the knobs. They were locked.

When I returned to the lobby, I spotted a man on a ladder. He was taking measurements from the ceiling down. He called them down to another man who stood by the window. The man on the floor wore white gloves. Sketches and paintings of a woman's figure were propped along the base of the room. Something about the sketches felt familiar. I stepped closer. The man on the ladder twisted around and yelled at me.

"Hey, you! You're not supposed to be in here," he said. "The building's closed for an installation."

I ignored his warning and stepped closer to the nearest painting. The image was of the back of a naked woman. Her hands were behind her, over her backside. The most striking thing about her was her silver hair.

"Who did these paintings and sketches?" I asked the man.

"One of the residents. We rotate the front gallery each month so everybody gets equal exposure."

"But there was a fashion show here last week, and this whole front gallery was empty except for a couple of mannequins."

"Yeah, funny how things work out. This guy raised the biggest stink about that show, and now he gets the lobby the month before the holidays."

"These are by Santangelo Toma, aren't they?" I asked. The man nodded. "Do you know where I can find him?"

"Sure. He's in his studio. Third door down on the right."

I thanked him and followed his directions. Like the rest of the hallway, the door to Santangelo's studio was closed. I tapped a few times and then tried the knob. It opened easily. Inside I found the artist sitting on a stool, staring at a half-finished canvas.

Smudges of charcoal were on his fingers and cheek. His clothes looked rumpled, as if he'd slept in them. Red suspenders were clipped to his loose-fitting trousers over a stained waffle-weave long-john top. His pork pie hat rested on the floor on top of a pair of shoes. His feet were bare.

Despite the cold temperature outside, the studio was warm. A small space heater was plugged into an outlet in the corner. A low table next to it held brushes and paints, a glass of cloudy water, and an assortment of oil pencils.

"Santangelo," I said, making my presence known.

He was startled. He crossed the room and pulled a tarp over the painting, but it was too late. I already knew who it was, and I knew what he'd done.

"That's Harper, isn't it?"

"I didn't make her do it. What's it to you?"

"You wanted the fashion people to be kicked out of the warehouse. You started a petition to get rid of Amanda. Explain to me how Harper being your model factored into that equation? If you got your wish and Amanda was evicted, you wouldn't have had access to Harper."

"She didn't want to be a part of that life anymore. She told me. I'm the only one who knew she was going to leave town."

"She told you she was going to Mexico?"

"She said she was going away. She felt bad because my paintings weren't finished. It was her idea for me to use the mannequins."

Instinctively, I turned and faced the part of the building where the installation was taking place. The woman's figure in the silver wig. That's why the silver wig was in the trash can the night Dante and I had come back. The image in the painting wasn't Harper; it was a mannequin.

I turned back and stepped closer to Santangelo. I put one hand out on his forearm. "The night of the fire, you took one of the mannequins, didn't you? From the lobby. You brought it in here."

"Amanda Ries's show made it so I couldn't concentrate. The only good thing that came out of it was meeting Harper. She said she liked the way I painted her. Real. Not like the fashion magazines. Not all airbrushed and Photoshopped. She said when it was all over, that's how she wanted to be remembered. But then everything got crazy, and she left."

"What do you mean, everything got crazy?"

"That photographer went after her. He wouldn't leave her alone. On her all the time, saying her career would be over if she didn't sleep with him. She couldn't take the pressure."

Dante had mentioned something about that when he first told me he knew Clive. A scandal. An underage model. A ruined career.

The Harper Ashton I knew was a sixteen-year-old girl on the edge of cracking. I'd seen it in her eyes. The demands of her job, the ill-fitting garments, the way she'd been treated more like an object than a person. She'd been too young to know how to deal with the demands of the industry, and she'd fled.

"Why did you try to burn the mannequin?" I asked.

He looked up at me. Whatever he'd hoped to gain by going against Amanda and Tiny had left him with little energy and even less spirit.

"After the fire, I knew somebody would find it in my studio and link me to the arson. I didn't need a lot of time, just a couple of days so I could finish my painting. But the investigators were poking around, and I couldn't concentrate. And I thought if somebody saw that mannequin, they'd think I was responsible. It was bad enough that I was so outspoken with my complaints and started that petition nobody wanted to sign. I might as well have put a neon sign over my head that said 'I'm a suspect.'"

"Detective Loncar is surprisingly understanding when it comes to stuff like that," I said.

Santangelo studied me. "You saw me. The night I set fire to the mannequin in the dumpster. I would have put it out, but you saw me. I had to get out of there. I couldn't risk my reputation, my show, my paintings. Not now."

I felt like I'd slipped into a world where people were commodities and creative pursuits were paramount. Somewhere along the way the humanity of life had been traded for fame and fortune, for false niceties that hid felonious rationalization. In all of my years in fashion, I'd never encountered people like this, who saw destruction and vandalism as justifiable when it came to protecting their art.

I backed away from Santangelo. His words said that he was sorry for what he'd done, but his actions told me he'd do it all again. If anybody was a victim in all of this, it wasn't him. It wasn't Harper. It wasn't me. It was Amanda.

I fled Warehouse Five for home. Santangelo had given

me more information than I could process on an empty stomach. After finishing the Neapolitan ice cream directly from the carton, I slowed down. Sure, the artist in residency had screwy motivation, but he'd done little more than try to protect himself. The person who had been out for himself all along was Clive.

I spun the empty carton of ice cream until I found Clive's number. He answered after several rings. I hadn't calculated the time change, but Tahiti was on the other side of California, so it was earlier than here, and I wouldn't have minded waking the British bum up.

"'Allo, darling. How are you? Enjoying a bit of a rest now that you've some time on your hands?"

"You might have fooled everybody else, but you haven't fooled me. I know about your history with the minor. Your career was almost destroyed. What did you offer to Amanda to get her to hire you?"

"Amanda gave me an opportunity to redeem myself, and I gave her legitimacy. My documentary would have done for her what *Unzipped* did for Isaac Mizrahi. She would have been more than a designer. She would have been a star."

"But you risked it all by making a play for Harper."

"I'd like to see you prove that bit of rubbish. Amanda and I had an arrangement. A couple of hours in the editing booth, and I'm certain to have a magnificent narrative of what happened."

"But there wasn't any show, and Amanda can't want your photos now."

"I have no loyalty to Amanda. I've spoken to editors at the major magazines, and there's extreme interest in what I shot. Ten different galleries are bidding on the opportunity to showcase the images, and the tabloids are talking six figures per image. Why shouldn't I take advantage of the situation? Exclusive footage of fashion in flames. Much better than what I might have gotten if the show went off without a hitch. You might say I got lucky."

"If the fire inspector can link you to the arson, I wouldn't call it lucky."

"Ms. Kidd, a photographer needs to know how to chase the light. That's what I did. Chased the light."

"And if someone had gotten injured in the process of you chasing it?"

"Then I'd have sold my film to the highest bidder and walked away. But alas, that wasn't to be the day I struck gold."

Again I thought of the strand of dyed-blond hair. "Is your hair color natural?"

"I hardly think that's relevant," he said.

"The police can link a person with dyed-blond hair to the fire," I said boldly. I didn't say which fire.

"A little Sun-In can hardly be called dyed. Now, if you're done with your interrogation, Ms. Kidd, I have sixteen swimsuit models waiting for me on a white-sand beach. You do know I'm in Tahiti, don't you? Where I've been for twenty-four hours. I've spoken to Inspector Gigger and Detective Loncar. If they were content to let me do my job, I suppose you should be too."

I made a fist and punched the cushion on the back of the sofa. "Thank you for your time," I said with as much cordiality as I could muster.

"Cheerio, lass," he said in return and disconnected.

Clive stood to make a lot of money from those photos, and if he'd been pressuring Harper for sexual favors, then he surely had no moral compass and would destroy

Amanda in the process of getting rich. If he was telling the truth about being able to sell the photos, then my suggestion that Amanda replace him with Dante had created a situation for her. It had made things worse. Amanda Ries might have fabricated some of her troubles, but as far as I was concerned, they were far from over.

I remembered the photos in the basement. Fine, I thought. Clive thinks he can make money by selling his photos? They'd lose all value once Nancie Townsend published Dante's photos in her new magazine. I'd show Clive the meaning of exclusive.

I called Nancie. "Nancie, this is Samantha Kidd."

"Samantha, I was just thinking about you. How's the article coming?"

"Better than expected. I'm pretty sure I can have something to you by tomorrow."

"Perfection. Do you have art?"

"I have art like you wouldn't believe."

"You're not toying with me, are you?"

"Here's what you need to know about me. When I say I'll deliver something, I deliver it. Deadlines are not a problem. Are you still interviewing other candidates for your full-time position?"

"There are a few people on my radar, but I tell you what. I'll blow them off until tomorrow at five. If your article is as good as you say it is, you've got yourself a job."

I brought the photos upstairs to the computer and sat down to write the exposé of all exposés.

SOME LIKE IT HAUTE

by

Samantha Kidd

The world of haute couture is fickle. Too long in the spotlight, and a designer can get burned. For emerging talent Amanda Ries, the burns didn't come from the spotlight. They came at the hands of an arsonist.

Details of the fire at the recent Amanda Ries runway show can be found in the newspapers and online, but what's missing from those reports is a description of the true stars of the show: the clothes. Why? Because aside from the first six runway looks, the audience didn't have a chance to see them. This reporter gained backstage access prior to the show and followed up with a visit to the showroom to document the full collection.

Formerly known for an ice-cream-sherbet color palette of All-American classics, Ries tried her hand at something new. Shades of orange, red, yellow, and silver decorated futuristic jumpsuits, motorcycle jackets, and kimonos. While other designers gravitate toward a post-apocalyptic future, Ries shows us an exuberant vision. Her woman of the future is strong, confident, and fashion forward, a merging of sixties space age and nineties minimalism with a dash of Harajuku thrown into the mix.

I chewed on my fingertip and read over what I'd written. So far, so good. Already I'd managed to plug my credentials and pull the rug out from under Clive's supposed exclusive by having art of my own.

Before continuing, I picked up the stack of images and flipped through them. It was about the clothes, not about me being in the clothes, so I ignored how I looked and focused on the garments. I selected four images and then prepared to send them. Here was the one flaw with Dante's shoot-on-film decision. What was I to do? Scan in these pictures and email them?

I hadn't talked to Dante since Tuesday night, when Loncar and Amanda had shown up. He claimed I went stiff as a board when Amanda showed up. And he took it to mean that I wasn't over Nick. He was right. But this didn't have to do with Nick. This had to do with an investigation that we'd started together.

I called him. "I need to email some of these photos that you took. How should I do that?"

"Whoa, slow down. No 'Hi, Dante'? No 'How was your day?'"

"Hi, Dante. How was your day?" I said.

"It was good. I took the bike to Jersey. Stared at the ocean for a couple of hours. Cleared my mind."

"Do you do that often?"

"Whenever I need some clarity. You should try it sometime."

"I don't have a bike."

"Anytime you want to go, all you have to do is ask."

I twirled a lock of hair around my index finger but said nothing.

After a few seconds, he spoke again. "So, what's this about photos?"

"I'm working on that article about Amanda, and I need the art. Your photos are on film, and they haven't been touched up."

"They don't need to be touched up. There's truth in them."

There was that word again. Truth. The same word Santangelo had used. It made me uncomfortable because I knew I'd been avoiding it. But there was no time like the present to acknowledge the truth about my own life.

"Can you come over tonight?" I asked.

"What for, Samantha?"

"So we can talk."

30

HALLUCINATION OF SILVER LAMÉ

I was wired with nervous energy, so I cleaned. Scrubbed the grout in the bathroom with a toothbrush and sponged down the baseboards. Even dusted the pages of the books on the bookcase. Fueled with romantic frustration, concern about Nick's father's health, and anxiety over the arsons around town, I might as well have hung drywall in the basement. The past week had taught me a lot about myself, and I was determined not to become one of those never-happy people even if it killed me.

By the time Dante arrived, I'd picked up a couple of smudges of dust and dirt on my sweater and plaid skirt. I didn't bother to change. He gave my outfit a quick glance but said nothing. I held the door open and let him in.

"I'd offer you something to drink, but your options are limited to water. Sparkling or tap."

He waved my offer off. "I have a feeling this isn't a purely social visit."

"It's semi-social. Come with me." I went upstairs to the spare bedroom and cued up my article on Amanda's show.

"This is an article about Amanda. It could lead to a job. I need your permission to use the photos. You'll get full credit, of course."

He fanned the stack of photos out and paused for a second over the one in the red dress. "You could have asked me that over the phone," he said.

"I need your signature."

"You didn't ask me here to get my signature on a release form."

"No, I didn't."

Dante leaned against the wall and crossed one foot over the other. He crossed his arms as well. The sleeves of his black leather jacket rode up, exposing his tattoos. "What's on your mind, Samantha?"

I chickened out. "Clive Barrington," I said.

"Clive? What's he done now?" He relaxed his arms, as though he'd been expecting a different subject.

"Someone set a fire in a trash can in front of my house." At the look of anger on his face, I continued. "I was able to put it out with an extinguisher before the fire department arrived. I found some ash in the bottom and looked at it under the microscope." I waved toward the Fisher-Price toy. "There was evidence of dyed blond hairs. You told me Clive dyed his hair. I thought it might have been him, except I confirmed he's been in Tahiti. He couldn't have set the fire."

He followed my gesture to the Fisher-Price microscope, and a hint of a smile tugged at his lips before he grew serious again.

"Clive Barrington is not a nice guy. He was always a part of the scene, not just the photographer, but on the party circuit. There was a rumor about him making advances toward the models, even those who were underage. He promised to help make careers. More than one mother looked the other way and left him alone with their daughters."

"Did any of the accusations stick?"

"Nope. The guy's like Teflon. He's an opportunistic bastard who looks out for himself."

"Does he have it in him to do any of this?"

"I wouldn't put it past him, but I can't see the upside. Clive Barrington doesn't do anything unless it benefits Clive Barrington."

"I called him earlier today. He's negotiating with some industry gossip magazines to showcase the fires. 'Fashion in Flames,' he called it. He said something about how a good photographer chases the light."

Dante leaned forward and flipped through the photos again. "If Clive let it be known to the right people that his footage was for sale, he could start a bidding war. I'm thinking he'd get six figures, maybe even seven. Fashion, emerging designer, arson. Could bring his name back into the limelight. Make him hot again. Make people forget about the accusations."

"There's a motive. And he was there. He had the opportunity. If only I could figure out how he started the fire."

Dante waved his camera. "There's a few more shots on this roll of film. I can develop them now if you want."

"Sure," I said.

"Come with me. It's been a long time since I had a photography assistant."

We went down two flights of stairs to the basement and entered the darkroom. Dante closed the door behind us. I turned to face him. He put his hands on my hips. I closed my eyes and stood there for a second, smelling cinnamon on his breath, before reaching up and moving his hands away.

"I appreciate you helping me with the investigation, but I'm not ready to do this," I said.

I wanted Dante to nod his understanding, but he didn't. He didn't walk away or say something cliché about being friends or toss out a light comment about timing or calling him if I needed a distraction. My words hung in the air with no acknowledgment that I had made a conscious decision to close this door without fully knowing what was behind it.

Finally, he spoke. "The new photos will be ready in an hour. No worries on using them. Email me the waiver. I'll sign it and get it back to you."

"Thank you," I said.

I left the room and went back upstairs to work on the article. After a short while, I heard footsteps downstairs. Seconds later, the garage door opened and shut, and a motorcycle drove away.

I emailed the finished article to Nancie with a note that photographer approval would be following soon. Next, I called Amanda's studio. Tiny answered.

"This is Samantha. I finished the article on Amanda. Any chance you or she would be available for a follow-up?"

"I told her that article was a bad idea, but her business is her business now. We parted company earlier today."

"She fired you?"

"I quit. If I don't get out soon, no amount of press in the world will save my reputation."

"But what about her? Amanda Ries Designs and her being on the verge of breaking out?"

"Sometimes you have to know when to cut ties from a sinking ship."

Amanda had surrounded herself with people to protect her from the details of running her business, and everybody was moving on. I wondered how she was taking it.

"Is Amanda there? Can I talk to her?"

"She's at Warehouse Five, wrapping up business with the insurance company. You can probably catch her if you get there soon."

Before she could hang up, I blurted out, "Oscar LeVay."

"Excuse me?" she asked.

"Have you paid him for the models at the show?"

"How is that any of your business?"

"I guess it isn't."

"That's right. Anything else?"

"Nope."

"Good. See ya around, Sam. I'd like to say it's been a pleasure, but that would be a lie." She hung up.

I stuck my tongue out at the phone and then looked up OLV Model Management and called the main number. A receptionist said Oscar was in a meeting and offered to take a message.

"This is Samantha Kidd. K-i-d-d. I'm working with Amanda Ries to resolve any outstanding issues related to her recent show. Do you know if Mr. LeVay received payment for the models yet? If not, I can arrange for a check to be delivered this afternoon."

"Mr. LeVay would probably want to talk to you about that. Hold, please," she said. She clicked me to a silent line for the briefest of moments, and then Oscar picked up.

"Tiny?" he asked.

"No, this is Samantha Kidd. I'm calling on behalf of Amanda Ries. Tiny is no longer with the company."

"Is this a joke?"

"No, sir. I'm helping Amanda clear up any outstanding issues that resulted from the fire, and I came upon your invoices. Where do we stand on them?"

"I'm not sure. Tiny claimed to have cut a check, but until I see it, I'm not going to believe it."

"Why don't I deliver payment in full? If I can verify that a second check has been cut, I'll put a stop payment on it."

He agreed. I verified his address and made arrangements to meet him before the close of business. I had a little over an hour.

Oscar was the only person still waiting for something from Amanda. It stood to reason that whoever was trying to destroy her wouldn't do so unless they got what they wanted. I'd give Oscar what he wanted and see what he did next.

My check from Amanda was still in my handbag. I scanned it into the computer and used the resulting jpeg to mock up a fake check with a suitably computer-looking font and a made-up account number. After a ten-minute diversion to look up the penalties for check fraud, I called Detective Loncar.

"This is Samantha Kidd. I'm about to deliver a fake check. I thought I'd tell you first."

"Ms. Kidd, intent to commit check fraud is a crime. Depending on the amount of the check, you could be looking at misdemeanor or felony charges. I thought you were smarter than that."

"Detective, I skewed the dimensions of the check by a quarter of an inch and signed it 'Diana Vreeland.' The routing number says 'gotcha' in a simple number-letter replacement code, and the currency of the check is listed as doubloons. I hardly think I could be accused of intent to commit fraud."

"Where are you?"

"I'm at my house, and I'm going to OLV Model Management. Oscar LeVay expects me to bring him a check on behalf of Amanda Ries."

"Don't do this, Ms. Kidd."

I retrieved the stack of photos that Dante had developed and set them by the door. Next, I showered and changed into a red turtleneck and matching wool cape, narrow black pants, and riding boots. I wrapped a plaid scarf around my neck, pulled on black leather gloves, grabbed a handbag, and left.

OLV Model Management was in West Ribbon. There was a noticeable change to the buildings once you passed through downtown. Houses looked more imposing, streets were cleaner, and new office buildings were interspersed with old ones. I parked close to the building entrance and let myself inside.

The first thing I noticed was the large glass vase that sat on the receptionist's desk. Instead of flowers, it was filled with bright oranges. I was so thrown off that I forgot why I was there.

"They're pretty, aren't they?" The receptionist smiled. "I love Clementine season."

"Clementines," I repeated. "Smaller and sweeter than oranges, aren't they?"

"Easier to peel too." She stood up and leaned over the vase, taking a deep breath over the vase. "They smell good too. Go ahead. Give them a whiff."

I tentatively stepped closer to the vase. From a distance of two feet away, I breathed in the scent. It took me back to the attack. Right before I was hit. I pushed away from the desk and yelled, "No!"

The receptionist, not willing to have a potentially deranged stranger hanging around her lobby, stood from her desk and very quickly escorted me to Oscar's office on the third floor. He appeared to be waiting for me.

"You must be Samantha. Come in," he said. "Care for a drink?" he asked. A fully stocked bar cart sat to the right of his desk.

Knocking back a shot of vodka wouldn't do much in the way of making me feel better. I considered asking if he had any meatball sandwiches lying around, but instead politely declined his offer.

Before diving directly into felony-committing mode, I set my belongings on the table and looked at Oscar's office. If hints to his personality were hidden in the room, I wasn't seeing them. The walls were lined with images of airbrushed models and not much more. His desk was immaculate, as were his bookshelves. Knickknacks were kept to a minimum, which seemed a nice gesture to the cleaning service.

Nope, if I was going to engage Oscar LeVay in any secret-spilling banter, I was going to have to play the cards I was dealt.

"Mr. LeVay, I wondered if I could trouble you for an opinion," I said. I eased the stack of Dante's photos out of the envelope. "You're a respected expert in discovering models. I recently had these photos taken. Do you think I have a future in the business?"

He took the photos and studied the one on top. The red dress. He flipped to the next one and the one after that. "You have a certain charm. Perhaps catalog modeling for the plus-size market."

"Excuse me?"

"Plus-size models are in the ten-to-twelve range. You're —how tall? Five six?"

"Seven. Five seven. And a half."

"A bit on the short side, and a little old for this line of work, but there's a place for big-boned girls like you."

My cheeks flushed red. The last time I'd checked, I was below the national weight average for women in the United States, but thirty seconds with Oscar, and I felt like an undesirable. Was this how he spoke to everybody who walked into his office asking about their chances for success?

Focus, Samantha.

"What about Harper Ashton? She's one of your top models, isn't she?"

"Was. I expected her to work for me for a long time. All she had to do was steer clear of the darkness of the industry, and she could have become one of the greats. Like Christie and Linda. Bring back the all-American look."

"I never thought about it, but she would have been perfect for Amanda's other collections. Before she went with Godzilla on the moon."

"You're right. She was to become the centerpiece of Amanda's collection. Classic American sportswear on a classic American beauty. The two could have helped each other, made each other famous. But then Amanda had this" —he waved his fingertips by his temples— "this hallucination of silver lamé. I tried to get Harper pulled from the show. She didn't need to be a part of Amanda's train wreck."

"You said 'was.' Isn't Harper with your agency anymore?"

"Harper disappeared after the show. I exhausted countless resources trying to make sure she wasn't injured or in any danger. There was a lot at stake. And then she sends a postcard from Mexico. No apology. No explanation. But I know who was behind it."

"Who?"

"Her sister."

"Harper has a sister?"

Oscar opened a leather-bound binder that sat on the corner of his desk and flipped through several pages of photos. He stopped on the second one from the end, pulled the glossy image out of its plastic sleeve, and held it up. "Her sister. Molly Diers."

31

PUTTING THE BAND BACK TOGETHER

THE FACE THAT STARED BACK AT ME WAS ONLY SLIGHTLY familiar. It was a different Molly than the one who needed my help to find an outfit for her in-laws' family gathering. The woman in the photo was airbrushed and glamorous in a minimalistic, late-70s way. Even in her modeling days, Molly Diers was into the bohemian look.

Oscar set the photo down and stared at the image. "Molly had the body and the attitude, but after the incident, she was over."

I rested my butt on the arm of the chair across from Oscar's desk. "What incident?" I asked.

"Molly took a job nobody knew about. It was a closed set and involved a bit of nudity. She was just a girl. There should have been a guardian, but there wasn't. Molly claimed abuse. Her mother, who denied giving permission for the job, came after me for sending a girl her age into an adult situation without supervision, and Molly dropped out of sight. The photographer left the country and only worked abroad until recently."

"Let me guess. The photographer was Clive Barrington."

"Yes." Oscar had been speaking from a collection of memories too strong to keep suppressed, but my interjection pulled him back to the present. He took in how I was resting on the arm of his probably very expensive office chair and stood to his full imposing height. I stood up straight, too, even though five foot seven and a half wasn't particularly imposing.

"Samantha, I believe you are here to deliver a check." He tapped the edges of my photos on his desk to line them up and handed them to me.

I tucked them under my arm while I felt around in my handbag for the envelope containing the check. As soon as he had it, I would be dismissed. Which was fine, because I had to get out of there.

I set it on the corner of his desk. He picked it up and looked inside. Satisfied with what a cursory glance told him, he looked up. "Let me know if you'd like help putting your portfolio together."

Sure. The next time I needed someone to pummel my self-esteem, I'd be sure to give him a call.

I threw the car into gear and peeled out of the parking lot. There was no way Molly Diers's arrival on my doorstep had been a coincidence. Especially now that I knew something had happened between Molly and Clive in the past. Add in that Oscar had represented Molly at the time of the incident.

Molly had dropped out of the modeling world, gotten married, let herself go, and gotten divorced. Three people who had a connection to Amanda's ill-fated runway show were at the same place at the same time. It seemed like someone was putting the band back together, and at the top of the list of potential organizers was Molly Diers.

According to the police, the only crime to be investigated was that of arson. Could Molly be guilty of setting the fires around town? She had motive: create a diversion to get her sister away from Clive Barrington. If Molly had taken note of the photos in the darkroom, then the fire at my house could have been a deterrent. Like the attack on me the night before the show. A message for me to mind my own business.

I drove to Warehouse Five. Traffic was light, and I arrived quickly. Two cars were parked in the lot: Amanda's little black coupe and a gold sedan with a dent on the rear passenger side. I pulled into the space next to Amanda's and got out.

Someone had propped the door open with a brick. I entered. Charred air perfumed the interior. I stood still and listened for the sound of voices. There were none. There was only the leftover smell of burnt building. My stomach turned. I moved forward.

The auditorium where Amanda's show was to have taken place was on the left-hand side of the building. I assumed that's where I'd find Amanda. I assumed wrong. The room was empty.

Although I'd been back at Warehouse Five to talk to Santangelo Toma, this was the first time I'd been inside the auditorium since the night of the show.

The room remained largely untouched from the chaos that had ensued. Chairs had been tipped over and pushed to the side to make way for patrons to flee. Scars of soot marred the walls. Burnt bits of rose petals crunched under my feet like discarded cornflakes.

Curiosity got the better of me, and I climbed up onto the catwalk. The original white plastic floor covering had melted in the fire and was fused to the damaged platform underneath. The smell was unbearable and probably toxic. I knotted my scarf around my neck and spun the knot to the back like a robber in an old western and then pulled the wool up over my mouth and breathed through it. Not much better.

I dropped down to all fours and ran my hand across the surface of the floor. I still didn't understand how the fire had started. I sat for a second and closed my eyes to recall what I'd seen both in person and on the videotape. Five models had walked down that catwalk before Harper. Nothing had happened to any of them. And then Harper had strutted her stuff, oversized kimono sleeves dragging along the floor behind her. The kimono went up in flames.

The *kimono* went up in flames. The flames started at the tip of the sleeves and climbed the garment.

I concentrated harder on the memory. The fire had been started at ground level. What was it? A trigger wire under the flooring? I scoured the floor for signs of platform tampering with low expectations for success. The fire inspector had been through here looking for this very thing, and it was a given he actually knew what a trigger wire looked like. If evidence had been left behind, it would have been found by now. By Gigger or Amanda or Tiny or an insurance agent who wanted to prove that someone else was responsible for the fire. The only thing left for me to see were melted plastic and long strands of metallic thread. The threads clung to the wool of my coat like sticky cobwebs. I'd seen these metallic threads before. They'd clung to my glove the night I'd felt around the macadam of the parking lot.

I reached down and peeled a strand of the metallic thread from my coat. I tried to tear it but couldn't. It wasn't thread at all. It was a thin, flexible wick. A few stray threads that matched those of Harper's kimono clung to the end as though the two had been connected.

And I knew. This was how the fire had been started. The long, barely visible wick had been attached to the oversized, dragging sleeves of the kimono and lit from backstage. The fire traveled the length of it until it reached the sleeve of the kimono. If I had a chance to examine that garment, I'd bet something had been hidden in the edges of the sleeves to make it combust.

Molly hadn't had the opportunity to tamper with Harper's kimono.

Tiny had.

The night I'd gone to Tiny about Harper's kimono, she'd been holding spools of metallic thread. She said she'd look at the ill-fitting garment if there was time. She hadn't been willing to make alterations. Her only concern had been making sure the wick remained intact. She'd planned all along to use that kimono to set fire to the show.

I tucked the cluster of metallic threads into my bra, not wanting to take a chance on them falling from a pocket. I climbed down from the platform and went backstage. The fire had destroyed most of the room, leaving an empty cavern. Anything that burned had been consumed by the flames, leaving exposed metal frames of the furniture. The walls looked like a graffiti artist had airbrushed on black soot marks, growing increasingly darker around the windows and the door.

The smell of the fire was stronger back here. Almost a week had passed, and just standing here, I could see the fire, smell the fire, feel the fire. The memory was as strong as it had been the night of the show.

That's when I realized I wasn't reliving a memory. A new fire had been set and was burning down what was left of Warehouse Five.

32

ANOTHER PRETTY FACE

Smoke trickled into the room from around a closed door at the rear. Worse, sounds came from inside. The same sounds I'd listened for when I first arrived.

I moved closer and reached out for the knob. The heat burned my fingers before contact. I dumped the contents of my handbag and turned it inside out and then used it like an oven mitt to grab at the knob. It opened. Smoke poured out of the door as it swung open. And then, something caught my ankle. I screamed and kicked away. The cloudy air made it difficult to see, but I squinted through the smoke to see what it was. A hand.

Tears clouded my vision. The scarf was no match for the smoke. I had to get outside where the air was clear. Phone, wallet, everything that had been in my handbag now lay scattered on the floor. All of that could be replaced. My life could not. Neither could the life of the person in the closet.

I looked down at the person on the ground. It was Amanda.

"Get out of here!" I called. I grabbed her hand and pulled her toward me. She fought my efforts.

She panted for air and coughed. I pulled the scarf down from my face so she could hear me. "You have to get out of here. Now!" I dragged her toward the back door. She stumbled through it and got about ten feet away from the building before collapsing onto the gravel, knees first. She turned over onto her back and coughed like a thirty-year smoker.

I stumbled away from the building and saw a car partially hidden down the road. It faced me. I ran toward it. My legs gave way halfway there. I fell. I scrambled back up to my feet. The engine started, and the car backed away.

Tiny's face laughed at me through the windshield. She was going to get away.

I dove onto the hood and grabbed the antenna. The car backed up, and I slid, my grip on the thin metal spoke the only thing that kept me tethered to the car. The antenna snapped off. Tiny twisted the steering wheel hard. My fingers hooked into the exhaust vents. Tiny's face was red with rage.

My body, sore from residual bruises and new injuries, couldn't take this for long. I couldn't even scream, my voice hoarse from inhaling so much smoke. Tiny arced the wheel hard and spun the car the opposite direction. I clung to the car. She cursed. The brakes slammed on. She reversed and drove, reversed and drove. I gripped tighter.

The car swerved into the woods. Silent screams tore at my throat. My cold fingers cramped. Branches scraped against me as she drove. The car skidded on a patch of sludge and spun across the road. My fingers released, and I flew off the car. I landed on hard, cold dirt, knocking the wind out of me. Tiny rolled her window down and smiled.

"Like I told you, you should have stayed out of it. Nobody would have suspected me. Not after people started digging into Clive's background with Harper's sister."

"You knew about that?" I choked out.

"Of course, I knew about it. I hired them both. I set the stage for little sister to follow in her big sister's shoes and for Clive Barrington to be suspect number one."

"You used Harper as a diversion? She could have been killed."

"Boohoo. The industry loses another pretty face. There's a hundred girls like her waiting in the wings." She spat out the window onto the cold, dry ground, barely missing my head.

"But why did you do it?" I asked in little over a whisper. Pain came at me like ice picks. I wanted to close my eyes and give up, but I had to hold on a little longer.

"Amanda was never going to be more than a two-bit designer, not with this collection."

"You convinced her to take a risk. You told her she needed a Hail Mary."

"All part of the plan. It was my money that backed her. My investment. I insured her company for ten-million dollars when I came on board. I needed her to believe that she was at the end of the line. All I needed was for the whole collection to go up in flames and be ruled an accident. Ten-million dollars paid to me."

"But why the rest of the fires? Why not just the one?"

"I got the idea when I saw the threatening letters."

I pushed myself up to hide the pain I was in. "Amanda—didn't tell you—about the letters," I panted.

"She didn't, but Oscar did." She smiled. "He demanded to know what was going on and threatened to leak the information to the media if we didn't pay him for the show."

"The rest of the fires—all to look—someone after Amanda?" My chest heaved and fell with each painful breath. "You made—fake letters—real?"

"I found the file on her computer. She made up the notes. Once I knew she invented them, I knew she'd never go to the police. It was perfect. But then you came along. You were never supposed to get involved. Why did you? She's your ex-boyfriend's ex-girlfriend. You should hate her as much as I do."

I coughed several times. Conscious and unconscious thoughts twisted in my mind. I had to fight to stay with her. I couldn't let her see how close I was to letting go, giving up, drifting into darkness. I channeled the Dread Pirate Roberts and addressed her while I conserved my strength. "Don't compare yourself to me. We're nothing alike." *I wouldn't be caught dead in men's jeans.* "You won't get away with any of this. You'll never see a dime of insurance money once the arson investor learns you're the person behind the fire."

"Prove it." She smiled at me. Tiny was no less intimidating when she smiled.

With every ounce of energy that I had left, I reached inside my bra and pulled out the cluster of thread that I'd found inside the warehouse. I held it up.

"This isn't thread like everybody thinks. It's a wick. You had it trail from the sleeves of Harper's kimono, and you lit it from backstage. When the fire caught up to the garment, it erupted."

Her smile froze. She opened the car door and stepped

out. I couldn't let her take it from me. This was the only evidence that I had.

I wrapped my arms around the tree next to me and pulled myself up. Lights from an oncoming car indicated we had company. Tiny's car blocked the road, but her lights were off. The oncoming car would have to stop. She turned around and shielded her eyes.

When she turned back to face me, I slugged her with everything I had in me.

And then the approaching car slammed into hers, knocking it off the road. The car hit Tiny, Tiny hit me, and we all crashed to the ground.

33

WRONG

My new hospital room was pink. Despite the charming hue, I wasn't any less freaked out than the last time I'd woken up in one. A curtain had been pulled shut between me and the other bed in the room, but I didn't know if I was alone or not. A few feet from the wall was a table that held a tray filled with food. If it wasn't a meatball sandwich, I wasn't interested.

A woman in scrubs printed with little crowns and tiaras walked in and checked my vital signs. "Are you up for visitors? A couple of people have been waiting to see you."

"Sure."

If I'd known my first visitor would be Detective Loncar, I might have given a different answer.

"Don't ask me what happened, because I don't remember," I said.

"Maybe I can fill in some of your gaps." He sat down in the chair next to the bed. "Tiny was arrested on suspicion of setting multiple fires around Ribbon."

"I was sure it was Molly Diers. She has a history with Clive Barrington. Did you know she's Harper's sister?"

"We knew all about Ms. Diers."

"You didn't tell me."

"She came to us in confidence. There was nothing illegal about her arranging for her sister to leave the country, but she wanted us to know in the event rumors about Harper's disappearance created a diversion from the arson investigation."

"That's where she got the sourballs. She took them from the bowl on your desk." It was the tiniest connection, but if I'd been paying attention, I might have realized it sooner. "How did you know where to find me? Last time we talked, you didn't say anything about suspecting Tiny. I only figured it out at Warehouse Five."

"When the report came in of the fire, I knew something was up. I called Inspector Gigger. He found the two of you on the ground about a mile from the warehouse. Nobody's sure how you got there considering the condition you were in. You were holding some metallic thread."

"It's what Tiny used as the wick to light the kimono. I should have noticed it earlier. It was on the parking lot macadam by my car. I thought they were cobwebs."

"Gigger recognized it for what it was. Amanda gave him permission to examine the garments at her showroom, and he found the same threads. We pulled in a computer guy who found an invoice on Tiny's computer for two dozen spools of microscopic metallic wicks. They were paid for with her personal credit card. It was enough to connect Tiny to the garments in the showroom, the garments at the show, and the garments that returned to the showroom. And the fire that took place two nights ago."

"Is that all?"

"No, that's not all. I thought you'd be interested in knowing that Ms. Anderson legally changed her name to Tiny several years ago. Prior to that, it was a nickname."

"What's her real name?"

"Clementine."

I closed my eyes. It was exactly the calling card I'd suspected, only Santangelo wasn't the culprit. Tiny had played off my injuries as if I'd made them up. Refusing to acknowledge that the attack had happened had been the perfect cover for her considering she was the responsible one. I tried to relax against the flat hospital pillow, but every position brought on pain.

"We followed up with Oscar LeVay too. Doubloons," he said, shaking his head. "That was a good one."

"What about Molly and Harper and Clive?"

"The statute of limitations on Ms. Diers's accusations has long since run out. Mr. Barrington is free to do as he sees fit. As for Ms. Diers and her sister, I think they're officially out of the business. Ms. Diers gave us an address for San Francisco."

Bohemian capital of the country. Figured.

"Ms. Kidd," Loncar said, "I appreciate your help on this. That last fire would have destroyed any evidence left. I'm not sure we would have put it together if it wasn't for you."

I swiped the tears from my face and tried to act like his praise didn't affect me. Loncar stood up and held out his hand. I shook it. He left the room.

Amanda walked in with a vase of orange roses. "I don't know how to repay you," she said. "You saved my life."

"You would have done the same for me."

"Let's hope it never comes to that." She set the flowers on

the table next to the bed. "Nancie Townsend called with a couple of follow-up questions to your article. When I heard about the new magazine, I told her she'd be a fool not to hire you." She picked at the corner of the hospital sheet and then stopped when she realized what she was doing. "If I were smart, I'd hire you myself. I'm looking for a new business manager."

"Amanda, don't take this the wrong way, but that's the worst idea you've ever had."

She smiled. "You're probably right." She pulled a pink envelope out of her handbag and tucked it under the vase of roses and then left.

Seconds later, Eddie took her place by my bed. I sat forward and looked toward the door. "Exactly how many people are out there?" I asked.

"I let them go first. It's all me until they kick me out." His blond hair was unkempt, pushed to one side and tucked behind his ears. He wore a Berlin concert T-shirt under a gray hoodie under a faded denim jacket. His cargo pants were weighted down by the contents of the pockets by his knees. He pulled two foil-wrapped items out of the pockets and set them on the table between us. The scent of meatball sub filled the room. "The commissary loves me. I've been buying meatball sandwiches every day just waiting for you to wake up."

I peeled back the paper and bit into the sandwich. Mozzarella cheese, soft meatballs, hard roll, yes. It was good to be alive.

"The stories in the waiting room describe a David-and-Goliath-style fight, but I'm having trouble picturing how it all went down. You were on foot. She was in a car. Care to tell me how you walked away?"

I looked at my hand and slowly made a fist. My skin was red, raw, and chapped, and a greenish-yellow bruise had formed by the knuckles. I ran my left fingers over the discoloration and remembered the moment when I'd slugged Tiny. A shudder wracked my body at the memory.

"Dude?" Eddie prompted.

"I guess she just caught me on the wrong day."

I didn't read Amanda's card until after Eddie had left. It was a generic Get Well, with balloons on the front and a sappy message printed on the inside. But under the message, in Amanda's neat handwriting, was Nick's name, followed by a New York phone number. I asked the nurse if I could use a phone.

Nick answered on the second ring. "Hello?"

"Hey Taylor, it's Kidd."

"Kidd," he said. "I didn't recognize the number."

If he didn't know about what had happened, he would soon, but that wasn't why I was calling. "I know you're probably busy, but I just called to tell you I was wrong."

"About what?" he asked.

I let a beat of silence pass before answering. "About cake. Nobody should have to eat cake without icing."

We spent the next forty-five minutes talking about this and that and nothing important at all.

It was exactly how I liked it.

FROM DIANE:

How many times does personal pride force us to follow through on something we don't want to do? And how often does that voice inside of our head tell us that maybe trying to change our lives is too hard, and that we should just stop trying and go back to where we were?

Samantha's new life is far from what she'd imagined: consulting for a designer she doesn't like, navigating the murky waters of her failing love life, and questioning if maybe she wouldn't be better off going back to her old job where at least she felt like she knew what she was doing.

If you're reading this, then you know those are the issues Samantha wrestles with in *Some Like It Haute*. And if you think about it, her leaving New York City before her first adventure in Designer Dirty Laundry was a pretty big lifestyle change. She's been in Ribbon, Pennsylvania for more than a year, and things still aren't quite working out for her. I don't know about you, but if that were me, I'd have a major freak-out/how did I get here?/go a little mad moment. And in the immortal words of Normal Bates, I guess we all go a little mad sometimes.

It's a good thing Dante was there to help Samantha through her dark days. Right? There are times I've felt like Samantha Kidd does: filled with self-doubt and second thoughts. For me, the unexpected, less safe choice usually works out well. For Samantha? You'll have to keep on reading her story to find out what trouble she lands in next!

Happy Reading,

Diane

P. S. Please consider leaving a review for this book. No matter how brief or how long, reader reviews make a difference. Thank you!

ABOUT THE AUTHOR

National bestselling author Diane Vallere writes smart, funny, and fashionable character-based mysteries. After two decades working for a top luxury retailer, she traded fashion accessories for accessories to murder. A past president of Sisters in Crime, Diane started her own detective agency at age ten and has maintained a passion for shoes, clues, and clothes ever since. Find out more at dianevallere.com.

ALSO BY

<u>Samantha Kidd Mysteries</u>

Designer Dirty Laundry

Buyer, Beware

The Brim Reaper

Some Like It Haute

Grand Theft Retro

Pearls Gone Wild

Cement Stilettos

Panty Raid

Union Jacked

Slay Ride

Tough Luxe

Fahrenheit 501

Stark Raving Mod

Gilt Trip

Ranch Dressing

<u>Madison Night Mad for Mod Mysteries</u>

"Midnight Ice" (prequel novella)

Pillow StalkThat Touch of Ink

With Vics You Get Eggroll

The Decorator Who Knew Too Much

The Pajama Frame

Lover Come Hack

Apprehend Me No Flowers

Teacher's Threat

The Kill of It All

Love Me or Grieve Me

Please Don't Push Up the Daisies

The Glass Bottom Hoax

Sylvia Stryker Outer Space Mysteries

Murder on a Moon Trek

Scandal on a Moon Trek

Hijacked on a Moon Trek

Framed on a Moon Trek

Warped on a Moon Trek

Material Witness Mysteries

Suede to Rest

Crushed Velvet

Silk Stalkings

Tulle Death Do Us Part

Costume Shop Mystery Series

A Disguise to Die For

Masking for Trouble

Dressed to Confess

<u>Mermaid Mysteries</u>

Dead in the Water

<u>Non-Fiction</u>

Bonbons for your Brain